The Hidden Light of Objects

Mai Al-Nakib

دار بلومزبري - مؤسسة قطر للنشر
BLOOMSBURY
QATAR FOUNDATION
PUBLISHING

مؤسسة قطر
Qatar Foundation

First published in 2014 by
Bloomsbury Qatar Foundation Publishing
Qatar Foundation
PO Box 5825
Doha
Qatar
www.bqfp.com.qa

Extract from Henri Bergson, *An Introduction to Metaphysics*. © 1973,
2007 by the estate of Henri Bergson. First published in 1913 by Macmillan
and Co. Reproduced with permission of Palgrave Macmillan.

A slightly different version of "Chinese Apples" originally appeared in *Ninth Letter*.

Reference to "Absolute" in Vignette III. Words and music by Green Gartside. ©
1984 by Green Gartside/Scritti Politti. Used by permission of Green Gartside/
Scritti Politti © 1984 by Ericton Ltd. Chrysalis Music Ltd. All rights reserved.
International copyright secured. Used by permission of Music Sales Ltd.

Reference to "The Word Girl (Flesh and Blood)" in "Bear." Words and music by
David Gamson and Green Gartside. © 1985 by Green Gartside/Scritti Politti. Used
by permission of Green Gartside/Scritti Politti © 1985 by Jouissance Publishing
Ltd. Chryssalis Music Ltd. All rights reserved. International copyright secured.
Used by permission of Music Sales Ltd © 1985 by WB Music Corp (ASCAP),
Gamson Songs (ASACP) and Jouissance Publishing (ASCAP). All rights on behalf
of itself and Gamson Songs. Administered by WB Music Corp. All rights reserved.

The poem "The Passage" from *The Pages of Night and Day* by
Adonis. English translation copyright © 1994 by Samuel Hazo. First
published by the Marlboro Press, Marlboro, Vermont. Northwestern
University paperback published 2000. All rights reserved.

ISBN 9789992195413

Cover by Holly Macdonald

Typeset by Hewer Text UK Ltd, Edinburgh

Printed and bound by CPI Group (UK) Ltd, Croydon, CR0 4YY

To my parents,
Nazha Boodai and Basil Al-Nakib

The mind has to do violence to itself, has to reverse the direction of the operation by which it habitually thinks, has perpetually to revise, or rather to recast, all its categories. But in this way it will attain to fluid concepts, capable of following reality in all its sinuosities and of adopting the very movement of the inward life of things.

Henri Bergson,
An Introduction to Metaphysics

The past is hidden somewhere outside the realm, beyond the reach of intellect, in some material object (in the sensation which that material object will give us) of which we have no inkling. And it depends on chance whether or not we come upon this object before we ourselves must die.

Marcel Proust,
In Search of Lost Time: Swann's Way

Contents

The Hidden Light of Objects

I

Blink and it's gone. But when it's there, it's expansive and may appear to cover a lifetime. It's a sand fountain or a bubble in a box. It's kept impeccable under glass. Sandwiched between one ordinary day and another, it's a night of school performances – a play or concert, band or choir. Walking, no, sauntering into school grounds at night, when it feels like we aren't supposed to be there, is an early experience of confident ownership not soon forgotten. Parents come later, after us, but, unlike us, they inch in timidly, on legs wooden with awkward reluctance. They don't really want to be there, though they are proud of us in advance for whatever it is we are going to do. What we do – a clarinet or sax, a song or dramatic turn – doesn't matter much. What matters, really, is the irresistible edge our school develops at night – the sexy shadow of the bubble against a pitch black concrete wall; hushed corners, invisible during the day, now deep, inviting pockets. As we march through the gates, heading toward whichever room we are supposed to be in, we think we hear something, a voice with an unexpectedly hoarse timbre that tickles the pelvis, maybe someone moaning. We look behind, to the left, to the right, nothing. But we can hear giggles about ready to explode into something grander. We feel the air pounding around us, like being encased in someone's racing heart. It feels like mischief.

It's dark and the December air is cool and crisp as a Chinese apple. Nothing big happens on this night, though electricity tingles all around us, and there are shapes in the shadows glued on like construction paper cutouts. The band plays, and then there's an extravagant performance of *The Frog Prince* or *Oklahoma!* It's background noise to the temptation strung all around like paper lanterns or popcorn, hanging there for the taking. We don't take enough, the arrogance of youth, and now look at us in our corner of the world, shattered in shards.

Once there was still mischief to be had and we were safe as crystal dreams.

~

Chinese

Apples

Japan is marvelous when you're ten. Japan is a street fair with white paper lights strung overhead. Japan is clip-clopping in wooden shoes through the twinkling night, your parents sauntering behind, pinkies linked, your sister, small as a dot on a map, safe in a stroller. Japan is a teal-colored kimono with a glorious peach sash. Japan is streets full of people you don't understand, laughing, pausing for breath, celebrating something unknown.

In Japan I was still the cherry blossom princess with a view of the world extended. That trip, a month and a half of our lives, now over two decades behind me. My father training to use complicated medical instruments, acquiring valuable expertise. My mother, my sister, and me along for the ride, suspended in a new place for a while, away from our desert home. That trip to Japan – an old man with Chinese apples, my sister the dot not falling, but almost. That trip to Japan – a razor on a window sill, four rice people in a box under glass. That trip – before the war that saves some of us, before my mother says, "My babies, my babies, take care of my babies." We were perfectly happy then, perfectly aligned. The four corners of a perfect square.

Every weekday morning in Japan, my mother would carefully place my four-year-old sister in a stroller and push her along the lovely tree-lined street near our apartment. The dot would squint her eyes at the sunlight squeezing through the trees, examining curiously the green and gold specks streaming across her arms. The dot wasn't very talkative then. She was thoughtful and maybe a little sad, like she knew something she wished she didn't. I didn't take her silence too seriously. I was content to be left alone, collecting the story objects I would share with her at night. The first week of our stay, my mother was preoccupied with the quotidian, figuring out where to get bread, butter, honey, vegetables, where to go in case either of us split our heads open, how to heat the water, how to pay for things. I didn't mind. I could never have enough time to myself. Like the dot, I too liked to be more quiet than loud. Surrounded by people speaking a language I didn't understand, the trip to Japan was ideal for expanding my collection. Without the usual tonnage of verbal distractions, I was free to devise my own.

I have collected story objects for as long as I can remember. Story objects are both objects and stories. Either the object or the story may come first. Most of the time, I select an object. It can be anything: a pouch of cat's-eye marbles, a sweaty scrap of blanket, Mr. Potato Head's smile, a small wooden bear, a pendant of a pyramid at Giza, a white cotton robe with blue flowers, a tiny packet of playing cards wrapped in fuchsia tissue paper. The object might appear in a room, under

6

the seat of a car, on a desert trip, behind a green trashcan, on a forgotten shelf. I don't necessarily have to save, own, or touch the object. Spotting it, even fleetingly, is usually enough. But once in a while I stroke the object methodically, my fingers creating an invisible grid around it, then cradle it possessively in my arms to feel the story enter me directly.

That's exactly what happened when I was eight and I decided I wanted to dig to China. I was slightly concerned because I imagined hell to be somewhere between China and me. But since it was daytime and the park full of adults, I was pretty certain nothing too serious could happen. Those were the days before smart bombs pinpointed children's heads, before oil was exchanged for lung cancer. Back then, a quick glance around the crowded playground was enough to quell any of my niggling fears about hell's creatures, its fire, its dank, fusty terrain. I started to dig at once. Past the loose top layer down to where it was damp, then wet, then thick as clay. The second I began to worry about worms, I felt something hard against the edge of my nails. I scraped away the wet sand around whatever it was and pulled. A fat, cobalt blue, partially melted, lopsided candle. It smelled awful, like stale, wet yeast. I brushed off the sand and ran home with the candle wrapped like a prize in my dirty red sweater. I washed it in the kitchen sink, but it still stank.

That night, I told the dot – a captive audience even at two – the story of the candle. It had been buried years earlier by Xiao Yong, a small boy in China. Like me, he had the idea of digging through the planet to get to the other side, to reach the place that wasn't China, to see if things were different there and how. He had dug far deeper than I and had needed

7

a candle to light the way in his dark tunnel. Fortunately, his family happened to be candle-makers, so there was no shortage of candles. From among the various colors he could have chosen – fire red, pus yellow, moss green, party pink, plum purple, mottled – he had selected blue for immortality and also because it had been the favorite color of his freshly dead brother. He knew he could face hell with his brother in his heart and his family candle in his hand. The blue candle had done well by Xiao Yong. It had glittered long past the center of the planet and almost all the way to the surface on the other side. But just when he thought he might actually make it, the slimy creatures of hell had caught a whiff of the candle's plucky little wick. Yong had been sucked into hell's fury and was never seen or heard from again. The blue candle had remained buried where he had last been. I flipped the candle over and, sure enough, found a stamp on the bottom that could only have been the Xiao family trademark. I kept the candle beside my bed and, on the one-year anniversary of finding it, lit it in honor of Xiao Yong and his brother.

Less often, I invent the story first. This happens mainly at night, in those rubber moments reserved for brains to bounce before falling asleep. It may also occur on a balmy day at the beach when the sun and breeze make me feel like I will stay young forever. Or while flying in an airplane through the clouds or looking down at them, thick and rolling, from above. In any case, seldom does the story come first, but when it does, the next day or two or three or the entire following week is organized around locating the object belonging to it.

Elias's story came to me this way, many years after Japan, after the Chinese apples and razor, but before the loss of the rice people, before the war. Late one night, I shared his story with my sister. A middle-aged man had decided to leave a green bottle by the side of the road. He had drunk from that same green bottle always. It was what he happened to be holding when they had come that morning to shoot his father and to pull his own life out from under him. For the next thirty-five years, Elias had funneled arak into that bottle religiously every night, then taken slow sips from it over the following day. By the time he was ready for bed, his bottle would be ready for a refill. One morning, Elias had awakened to find his bottle empty. A confused bird or gust of wayward wind through the window might have knocked it over in the night. His routine had been disrupted, but he had continued to take sips from the empty bottle that day because he hadn't known how not to. Every sip of air had surprised him, lacerated him with a loss he had for so long squeezed out of his memory with the help of distilled aniseed. By nightfall, Elias had felt less a man than an animal. He had collapsed onto the blue and white tiled floor of his apartment, his knees and hips melting away. He had moaned like death for twelve lingering hours. Every moan had stood for one thing he would never have because his people's land, his father's land, his land had been filched: a wife with magnolia skin, a child with delicate fingertips, an orange grove, a shattering blue sky, pine nuts in a bowl, bougainvillea climbing the garden wall, evening cicada songs, green bottles for clear water, a patient, persistent peace. The next morning, the first thing Elias had done when he got up was to take the empty green bottle to the side of the road and leave it there. The time to bottle loss had come to an end for this man. It was time to remember, not to forget.

It took me two full weeks to find the green bottle on the side of the road. But as always with story objects, it was there, patiently waiting for me.

There is never only one story per object. An object's stories are without limit, infinite. Like a fingerprint, my story will never exactly match anyone else's or even another one of my own about the same object. Though just as fingerprints may differ from each other by a tiny whorl to the left or right, such is sometimes the case with stories. A man in Gaza today might find the same story object as a man escaping on a ship to New York in 1941; a woman in southern Beirut the same as a woman in Dresden; a child in Basra the same as a child in Warsaw. Their stories will slide into each other, commingle, cohabit, connect in every way but one. Story objects are cobwebs across space and time. When you think it has never happened to anyone else ever before, a story object proves you wrong, though you won't always know you have been proven wrong. Most people's stories are hidden away. Objects may provide the only chance – unlikely, impossible though it may be – to unravel kept secrets.

We encountered the old, old man on our fifth morning in Japan. Without words, my mother, my sister, and I would ready ourselves for our daily walk, finding a home in a newly acquired habit. The dot, normally quiet anyway, would silently allow our mother to change her into a pretty summer dress and plop her into the stroller to wait until it was time to go. While neither stubborn nor prone to the usual obnoxious tantrums of children her age, the dot nonetheless would insist on one non-negotiable point: she had to carry a small purse wherever she went, and her purse had to match her outfit. She would choose from the four or five little purses she had acquired in her short life and then allow my mother to select clothes to match. My sister was not terribly impressed with conventional toys, but putting choice objects into her purse and then tenderly taking them out again one by one was a game that kept her amused for hours. My mother's discarded lipstick; a stone she had found mysteriously under her pillow; a tiny Kinder Egg teepee; a packet of mini colored pencils; a postage stamp-sized note-book full of her scratch 'n sniff stickers, one per page; a barrette threaded with sky blue and yellow ribbons; a pendant of a four-leaf clover preserved in resin; a silver bead; a plastic compass so she would never get lost; five bottle caps from five different sodas she was not allowed to drink; a Grover Band-Aid for her thumb, which she sucked raw. These objects defined the dot's existence then, and she felt secure and happy carrying them around with her everywhere she went. Waiting quietly in that stroller, sucking on her right thumb, clutching her purse tightly with her other hand like an Italian *nonna* on a tram, staring at the world with limpid black eyes, my little sister made me love her, made me realize this kind of love could create like magic and destroy like death.

That fifth morning we followed the same path we had on the four previous days: a left at the gate and straight down the tree-lined street. It was an extraordinarily quiet street, every sound hushed by the leaves, like walking through snow. There were never any other mothers or children around. We had not crossed paths with anyone yet and were not anticipating any different that morning. But about twenty meters into our stroll, we noticed that, unlike before, a gate to one of the

11

homes along the street was wide open. Our pace slowed automatically and we all peered inside, three curious floating heads. The dot even stopped her incessant sucking. The old man glided out from behind a tree like a ghost. My mother jumped and made a strange, small sound with her breath. I screamed. Only my sister looked on unperturbed. The old man went directly for the dot, petting her on the head as if she were a baby goat and cooing at her. Cooing and sighing, cooing and humming, cooing and petting. *Hmmmmmmm. Aaaaaaah*. His great, big toothless grin seemed to stretch his fragile face to the point of tearing.

It went on for what felt to me like hours. At first my mother seemed disconcerted. The veins in her hands stood out so I knew she was tense and unsure what to do. My mother never, ever showed us her worry, but the raised blue veins on her butter smooth hands were the sign I had learned to look for. Her concern quickly passed. My mother adored old people; through them she adored her dead parents. Soon enough she was smiling encouragingly at the old man, nodding and cooing back at him. After he had had his fill of the dot, he signaled for us to wait. We waited, quiet as time. The old man returned with a round object wrapped in laser purple paper. He placed it carefully in my sister's open hands. The dot smiled up at the old man, the kind of smile that reminds you of all the joy that survives in the world despite lost children and dead parents, despite cancer and war. He bowed gracefully, withdrawing behind the tree through which he had seemed to materialize earlier.

My mother kneeled down and unwrapped the object in the dot's lap. It was a fruit we had never seen before, larger than an apple, about the size of a grapefruit. It was round and yellow like the leaves of a neglected book. It had the stem of an ordinary apple only shorter. When we got home, my mother washed the fruit as carefully as a prayer, dried it with a pink-edged kitchen towel, and sliced into its crisp white flesh with a sharp black ceramic knife. The juice from the fruit sprayed into my mother's brown eyes, and she giggled like a little girl. She gave me a slice, then one to the dot, and then bit into a slice herself. It was crunchy and sweet and full of fragrant water that dribbled down my chin. The dot and I looked at each other with raised eyebrows, delighted at the new taste on our tongues. We shook our heads back and forth like the old man had done, cooing at each other and laughing hard, with our mouths wide open and our heads thrown back, for the first time since we had arrived in Japan. My mother continued to slice the fruit in threes, and we ate it slowly, slice by slice, till there was nothing left but a stem and a few brown seeds.

The next day, the gate was again wide open. Again we slowed down, and again the enchanting old man appeared as if from thin air. Again he cooed. Again he petted the dot on the head and cheeks for a very long time. My mother and I stood back and watched him. The dot had him mesmerized, his big toothless grin something to behold, an addition to the universe we would never forget. Again he signaled us to wait, and again he returned with a round object wrapped in purple paper. A final pat, an elegant bow, and goodbye. This routine continued every single weekday we remained in Japan.

The old man is certainly dead now. Even then, twenty-five years ago, he was old. Not old the way grandparents are old, but old to the point of paper thinness. As papery thin as the white lanterns strung overhead at the street fair. As papery thin as a dying petal of bougainvillea, no longer shamelessly pink, not even pale yellow, but transparent, ghostly, fading to nothing. Who did the old man see when he looked at the dot? Who did my little sister become for him? A daughter? A sister? A friend? What had happened to his version of the dot? She had to be lost, missing, a space in need of filling. A feeling to be remembered or maybe forgotten. A day at the playground in the sunlight or a picnic under a canopy of trees or a wade in a shimmering forest stream. Who was she? Where was she? Inside my sister? Inside the fruit he presented to us so carefully wrapped?

We never learned the name of the fruit while we were in Japan. About a month after our return home to Kuwait, we learned its name from our neighborhood fruit seller Ali, a scrunched up man from Iran who had fled the revolution. The magic of our trip, a secret shared by the four of us, was already tucked tightly in a pocket, to be mostly forgotten for years, remembered unexpectedly during war or before death or on the night of a mid-Ramadan moon. Ali called my mother "Um Ali," mother of Ali, because he believed the dot, with her short, nearly blond curls, was a boy. All through my mother's pregnancy, Ali had been cheerfully adamant that she was carrying a boy. He had made her promise to name the baby Ali, after his son. When my sister was born, my mother didn't mention Ali's mistaken prediction; she didn't want to break his heart. Ali had left his son behind in Iran with his wife. Like the old man from Japan, he too would sometimes linger over the dot. "Ali! You're bigger today. Much bigger than last week." But Ali's focus would quickly shift from the dot to his own little Ali, for whom, soon, soon, any day now, he would pay someone large sums of money to bring over from Iran.

Ali's shop was tiny, no bigger than an average-sized bathroom. But it had a higher-than-average ceiling and Ali used every bit of shelved wall space to display his fruits. Fruits from Colombia. Fruits from Chile. Fruits from Lebanon. Fruits from India. Fruits from New Zealand. No fruits from Iran. "On principle," he would say. My mother pointed up at a shelf close to the ceiling. Ali slid onto his ladder like a lizard and brought down the box. It was stamped "China." It was full of purple tissue paper. The dot and I sucked in our breath together.

"These are Chinese apples, Um Ali. Have you ever had them before?" He pulled out a round, familiar yellow fruit from the box.

My mother, as excited as the dot and me, inquired, "Are you certain they are Chinese, not Japanese?"

"Chinese, Japanese, what's the difference? These are the apples that grow over there. We don't have these in Iran. We don't have them here. As far as I know, these apples have come from China, but maybe they grow in Japan too. Maybe in Japan they're called Japanese apples."

"We'll take the box."

Four Chinese apples. Carefully wrapped in purple paper. Never quite as yellow or as crisp as the old man's offerings to the dot. Nonetheless, every week till she died my mother bought a box of them from Ali, whose son, by then a man, never arrived despite all that money changing hands.

*   *   *

Each weekend in Japan, my father would plan some great adventure for us. Since he was busy all day, all afternoon, all night during the week, he saved the weekends for "his girls" – my mother, the dot, and me. We would spend most of the time wandering around Tokyo, visiting the markets, pointing at squishy food that looked like worms or eyeballs, daring each other to taste the samples generously offered. I would hold my little sister's hand and we would walk ahead together. Every once in a while, we would glance back over our shoulders at our parents happily swinging their clasped hands up and down like children do. On one of our weekend outings, I discovered that machines that looked like they should have gumballs in them instead contained little colored pendants imprinted with animal images. I was born in the year of the dog, so the machine spat out a blue enamel pendant attached to a blue string with a silver image of a dog on it. It seemed too precious to have come out so unceremoniously and for the price of a gumball. I was enthralled. Even the blue string was special. Not yarn or thread but a strong, robust string worthy of the pendant. An important story object.

I discovered also that in department stores women dressed like princesses bowed in elevators. They bowed as we entered; they bowed as we exited. It made the rides up feel like flights into the sky and the rides down like falling into clouds. One of these elevator trips landed us in the children's department. My parents wanted to buy me a kimono. The loveliness of the cloth – blues tinged with pinks, purples with pale yellows, greens with sharp oranges – plunged me into a garden. I was overwhelmed by the swish of silks; even the modest cottons

16

had me captivated. I remember wanting to bury my face in the colors, to inhale the texture deep into my lungs, to hold it there forever. My mother picked out an exquisite and unusual teal-colored kimono printed with peach and white blossoms. The approving assistant brought out a matching peach sash, or *obi*. A pair of greenish, wooden *geta* completed the ensemble. I was in heaven. For the first time I felt beautiful, like my mother. I refused to take the kimono off, and my mother said she didn't blame me. I felt like the women in the elevators. I bowed to the assistant, who bowed back. I didn't know then that the kimono would also become an important story object, containing in its billowing sleeves my mother's love for me and her youth and beauty too.

But the most important story object from Japan was the red box with the glass lid and the four rice people inside. I found it in a dusty old shop, small, barely there, like Ali's room of fruit, with shelves all the way up to the ceiling, but lined with velvet, red or blue or maybe green, and piled with clay vases, rolled-up parchments, books of all sizes, porcelain sculptures of horses or dogs, silver dishes, and old clocks. Tucked away in this small, dark space, with the light slyly filtering through and the dust hesitating in the air, I found a small box. It was my ultimate story object. The story found the object this time because for about a week I had been thinking about these perfect four. I never dreamed they would turn up on one of our weekend outings together, in a tiny red box my parents agreed to buy me.

The box and four figures began to arrive in my head one day, while we were waiting for the old man to return with his purple-wrapped present for the dot. What I saw first was a

17

small, square piece of glass. Then nothing for several minutes. Then, abruptly, a red square box – an inch and a half by an inch and a half by half an inch – its lid the small glass square. Then, inside, one by one, like tiny stars in a velvet sky, the four appeared. Four members of a family. Four friends. Four together and sometimes apart. Four seconds before a long fall down, before a razor's cut, before death. Four small grains of rice, painstakingly painted, eyes and ears and hair and smiles, necks and noses, brows and bosoms. Four rice people together in a box. Perfection under glass, still, silent, secret. Among those shifting four, sometimes Xiao Yong. Among them Elias, Ali, sometimes the old man. My sister. My mother. My father. Me. The four corners of a perfect square. Four specks of rice laid out on a velvet bed, like stars in a velvet sky. With the rice people, the story came first. Not just one story. All the stories. Each and every story together but also laid out, separate, not touching. The story of these four was together and apart, remembering and forgetting, shapes and cuts. The story of these four was the sustaining secret of a perfect square. Swishing silks and clomping *geta*. A cooing old man and Chinese apples. Before stolen objects and collapsing lungs. The story of these four was an impossible forever in a box under glass.

The box of four, more precious to me than pearls or rubies or emeralds from India, was carried back to Kuwait, back to the land of desert and sun, with care, with love. A gift to me from my parents, so young then. Their love, too, under that glass, for me, for each other, for the dot. I kept them safe in the top drawer of my oak dresser, in the bedroom I shared with my sister, safe with Mr. Potato Head's smile, a pendant

18

of a pyramid at Giza, a paper-wrapped razor. Safe but not forever, nothing safe from war.

On one of our weekends in Japan, my father gathered us up and took us to a town with a spa famous for its steaming, therapeutic waters.

"These waters are supposed to heal aching muscles, to rejuvenate tired limbs, to recuperate weary souls. Do you want to try? Just up to your knees." The dot and I did not want to try. We did not want to lower ourselves into the dark, scalding waters. We didn't know what was down there, deep in the bubbling darkness. We weren't going in. Wide-eyed shakes of the head. Vehemently, no. We watched our parents in the waters, closed eyes, slow sighs, small smiles, pink cheeks. We waited for them on the wooden planks outside the soaking pools, the dot with her purse patiently emptied, refilled, emptied again, telling her version of a rosary, and me, with my story objects, telling mine.

Back in our room, the balcony, the scene of disaster averted, of sadness snatched back, overlooking a verdant valley, an Asian Ireland. One side of the perfect square momentarily loosed, fragile, almost broken, falling but not fallen. The dot standing between a damaged rail and the end of time. Small, exposed, with a wide, deep space below, a valley and a certain end. She was curious, surveying the lushness, the mossy green-ness matching the light that flecked her arms during our morning strolls. The valley below, like the trees above us, tingeing the light the color of freshness, of spring and things newly born. It could be that what I really remember is the photograph capturing the moment after the disaster averted.

A photograph of my mother with the dot enfolded in her arms. My mother's panicked eyes glazed with somber relief. The dot mostly oblivious but aware slightly of my mother's pounding heartbeat against her little back, of the raised veins of her butter hands against the dot's cheeks. What made my father rush to his camera then, at that moment, the moment immediately after his daughter was snatched back from the great fall down through the damaged rail, down to the valley below? What was it exactly he sought to capture, to put under glass? By the skin of, on the brink of, back from the edge of, clinging to? My mother had that same look in her eyes, later, dying, on the brink of, on the edge of, clinging to, but not able to be saved by the skin teeth of. My mother into my sister's ears then, "My baby, my baby, my baby." Her whispered mantra an aural ghost of the future, dying, dying, four seconds before death, "My babies, my babies, take care of my babies."

Her death came, poisoned lungs, ten years after the war that saved some of us. After her, fish died, millions, buildings fell, people fell, thousands. And more wars, always, for us, here, war after war after war. Four seconds before the end, what did they remember? Before jumping off, before being blown to bits, before bombs on heads from above. What did they remember? *Hmmmmmmm. Aaaaaaah*. Cooing can help, and sighing and humming. He is most certainly dead now. And Ali's son, the one who never came. And my mother, with them, dead. Each with a packet of four seconds before, if they were lucky or, perhaps, very unlucky. Four seconds to pack forever into forever after. Did she remember him? Did he remember us? Will we remember him? We will remember her.

How could we not? "My babies, my babies, take care of my babies." Who was she saying it to? To my father, whose intricate medical instruments were of no use in the end? My bewildered father, whose camera, decades earlier, had captured unbearable terror, undiluted intensity, under glass? To the humid hospital air? To the small brown birds on the sill, chirping in the silence before death, impossibly alive, for now? To her dots, no longer so little, but always little to her, remembering our ten tiny fingers, our ten tiny toes intact? Nobody can take care of us now with fish dying and buildings falling down. Did she know that? Is that why she said it? Defiance in the face of unbearable terror, undiluted intensity. Defiance under glass. But our mother dead anyway.

The last story object I collected in Japan was a razor. From the day we moved into our ground floor apartment home away from home, I was fascinated with the abandoned window above my bed. It was high above, too high to look out of. An odd window, long and narrow, without a screen, without a latch of any sort. Even light seemed hard pressed to filter through, the glass pane tinted orange-beige or rust brown. My mother hated the room. It was small, with barely enough space for a narrow cot, mine, and a corner cot, foldaway, the dot's. My mother seemed squished in that room. She detested its thick, mustard gas gloom. But with the door shutting everything out, the dot and I, feeling like we were floating inside the belly of a submarine or spaceship, loved it. I had tried a number of times to lift the dot above my shoulders, to have her peek outside the window, to see the adventure that had to be beyond the orange, the beige, the rust, the

21

brown, but she was too heavy for me, my shoulders too unstable, my arms too weak. So we dreamed beyond the glass pane.

On our last afternoon in Japan, with my harried mother gathering bits and pieces of things to pack away, my father trying to help, and my sister, disturbed by all the hullabaloo, hiding in my parents' bed, I pushed one of the kitchen chairs into our little room and shut the door. Carefully, ever so, I balanced the rickety chair on my cot below the window and myself, circus girl, on the chair. I could reach the sill, but I still couldn't see out the window. It was enough for me. I ran my index finger along that coveted sill, slow, slow as stones. Halfway, I had to stop to move the chair further along the bed. My finger was covered with a fine, white dust, like powdered sugar. I tasted it. It tasted like the smell of the ground after a duststorm washed away by a rainstorm, the smell of Kuwait in November or April. Balanced again, I continued to run my finger across slowly, lulled. But then, all of a sudden, an icy feeling, quick, sharp. I drew my finger away. Powdered then bloodied. A cut. Again, I tasted. Dusty rust. With my other hand, I reached up and found the culprit, a razor half-covered in gray paper marked with red script and my blood. I wrapped the razor in the paper, came down off the chair, and pushed it back into the kitchen. I washed my finger and put a Band-Aid on it. I didn't tell my mother or my father or the dot about my cut. I pocketed the razor and took it back home with me.

The razor's story was one of losing, being lost, loss. Its story the story of remembering and goodbye. Touching that sill was saying goodbye and, at the same time, inscribing myself there, in its lonely, orange light, forever, though I must have half-realized, even then, the impossibility of that. Goodbye to Japan, my mother, my story objects, which would never come as thick and fast as they did during that quiet trip without language. Goodbye to the kind of love that, even in the face of death, continued to love and to worry about her babies, the dots she made, her stars in a velvet sky, hers in a box under glass. The razor was remembering, remembered, memory. The old man's fallen daughter or sister or friend. A cobalt candle, land lost, a son left behind. It was the blue and white robe my mother used to wear in the evenings before bed or at the breakfast table while reading the papers, which now the dot – all grown up, a facsimile of my mother, loveliness and grace, limpid black eyes – wears and wears. It was a packet of tiny playing cards wrapped in fuchsia tissue paper found on a shelf after my mother's death, just there, inexplicable, but undeniably hers. It was all those objects that make me sick when I see them, that cut me every time, because the one who chose them, lived with them, used them, adored them is dead now, just dead.

And when the objects were lost, stolen from the top drawer of my oak dresser during the war of oil and cancer, I was sad, like sweetness had been sucked out of everything. Where are the stolen four now? Do they remember me like I remember them? Before the end, Chinese apples.

II

Almost every April, a group of teachers would catch spring fever and plan a trip to the island of Failaka for their students – seventh or eighth graders, sometimes even high schoolers. We were thirteen when they piled us into a ship, out in the sea breeze for a day, at a time in our lives when a day was really worth something. Getting to Failaka was easy. The water must have been a crystal blue tinged green, not sullied, as it would become, with fish still relaxed close to shore. I remember the marble ruins, marks of the great Alexander. I remember the temple of Icarus, named for the son who flew too close to the sun. I remember the citadel, the cemetery – Kuwaiti sand, Greek bones in part – and the artifacts. I didn't know that *fylakio* was Greek for outpost. I didn't dwell on the implications of an ancient Alex in my blood. Failaka, at that instrumental point where the Tigris and Euphrates pour into the Gulf, an outpost indispensable to Alexander's global plans; young Alex, dead in Iraq at thirty-three. I didn't realize Failaka had been inhabited for centuries, at least four before zero, before, that is to say, Christ (another goner at thirty-three). But Failaka, like Icarus, like all of us, would fall. It would be occupied, its inhabitants chased out, their belongings on their heads, its beaches and its unexpectedly green terrain sown with mines. Icarus, reaching for the sublime, for a beyond his father could see past and

25

warn against, falls. His leg, clawing like a crab's, the last appendage above water, of no use. Icarus falls, cracks like an egg. All of us on that ship oblivious of his fall, of Failaka and its fall, and of ourselves, so many Icaruses, falling out of a dazzling sky.

~

Echo

Twins

Mama Hayat stopped breathing in the early evening, around the hour the sun turns the sky above the horizon the color of a bruise. The twins, hovering over their mother's declining body for days, tabulating the signs of her approaching end in the slightest twitches of her fingers and toes, noticed the instant her chest sank and failed to rise again. The young men gulped air twice in quick succession. The first gulp, understandably, expressed shock. While they knew their mother had been battling something these last few months, they had never allowed themselves to think that whatever she had might kill her. The second gulp, however, was irregular. Had anyone else been in the room to hear it, they might have considered it indelicate, possibly conspiratorial. Together with the rapid glances fired between the twin pairs of glinting black eyes, the second gulp could have been interpreted as joy.

That would have been a mistake. Eighteen-year-olds Mish'al and Mishari adored their mother. They were not happy to see her dead. They were devastated and, soon

29

enough, would begin to feel as if their skin were being peeled off slowly, lemon and salt rubbed into their exposed flesh. The feeling of losing a mother. But there was a secret hidden beneath the ribs of their family, and their twin hearts beat wildly with excitement because they realized the age of vagueness was over. That second gulp was an acknowledgement between brothers that the years of living under the shadow of a mystery, a childhood of unanswered questions, nearly two decades of stories impossible to pin in place, were done. The golden age of certainty – what they craved more than any other thing, even more than a father – would dawn. They believed, as they had been led to believe by Mama Hayat herself, that their mother's death would bring with it disclosure.

The family secret would be revealed.

Truth be told, the twins had not suffered in the early years of their childhood. On the contrary, until they were eight, they believed in the full glory of their lives. They lived with their mother in a typically Kuwaiti mud brick house overlooking the glowing waters of the Arabian Gulf. The thick, mostly windowless outer walls enclosed a charming open courtyard overrun with pots of purple and yellow flowers reaching out to the sun all day, then tightly folding up their petals in late afternoon. In the middle was a sheltering *sidr* tree ringing with sparrows and red-vented bulbuls. Bright rooms with windows and paned doors opened onto the central courtyard which could be seen from every corner of the house. The courtyard was bordered by a shaded, arched corridor surfaced with tiles hand-painted blue, green, and rust. Burnished teak beams, likely scavenged from one of the dhow-building yards nearby, supported the roof.

When it rained in late November, Mish'al and Mishari would sit huddled close together on one of the wooden benches along the corridor and watch as muddy rivulets streamed down from the *sidr* tree to the four corners of the courtyard where the drains were located. It looked to them as if the tree were growing new roots before their eyes. They would convince each other that the normally placid tree, aggravated by the unfamiliar thunder and rare deluge, was planning to take over their home and that, in the dead of night, its roots would twist around their mother's neck, their necks, and pop their heads off. Screeching with self-induced terror, the boys would jump off the bench and, each trying to get ahead by pulling back the other's *dishdasha* collar, they would scramble madly to the kitchen where Mama Hayat could always be found preparing something unusual for them to eat – chickpeas and pine nuts simmered in molasses or crabs poached in red lentil broth.

The kitchen, like every other room of the house, was cooled by wind tunnels designed to suck in the sea breeze. Even during the hottest days of August, the temperature of their home remained tolerable, even pleasant, the tiles refreshing under their cracked bare feet. The sound of the wind wending through the rooms and corridors was constant, a familiar fourth member of their household. The family slept together upstairs in a loft with paned doors that opened onto a terrace. On summer nights, when the wind was still and the tempera-ture hot enough to boil a pot of water, they would pull their mattresses out onto the terrace to sleep. From there they could

31

see the silent black sea, flat as a mirror. When they looked down over the low terrace ledge, they could make out the shadows of their tree, and the brothers, feeling vulnerable in the night, never forgetting for an instant what the roots of that *sidr* tree might be capable of, would glance down frequently just in case. Spending the night on the terrace under the stars was part of summer life in Kuwait. In the days before air conditioning, everyone slept out on their terraces during the long, scorching months. It was like a slumber party to which the whole country was invited. Mama Hayat would tell her boys stories late into the night, making them giggle and gasp, allowing them to eat sticky, almond-stuffed dates in bed. They would fall asleep to the sounds of their neighbors' snoring, their furtive whispers in the night. The sleepy trio would often blink open their eyes at exactly the same moment too early the next morning, stirred awake by the rose glow of the sun peeking over the terrace wall.

Mama Hayat told stories. She raised her boys under a steady drizzle of tales. A drizzle in the desert was a luxury the twins never took for granted. Mama Hayat's tales were often amusing. In her kitchen, as she was busy concocting meals nobody else would think to put together, her stories would gush out forcefully, like black oil. In the middle of frying and grilling, boiling and baking, their mother's narratives would rise and rise, so wildly hysterical they made the twins fall to the floor and roll around the courtyard, two rubber balls of uncontrolled laughter. But by late afternoon, especially right after siesta, Mama Hayat's accounts would turn sad. She would speak in elusive fragments, puzzle pieces the boys would grab on to and try, over weeks, months, even

32

years, to put together. Only rarely could they forge sense out of her afternoon words, a procession of slow, solemn beetles. She would say things like: "Ships arriving and sailing past. Yellow follows no logic. A mountain of courage. Lost compass. Two in a drum left behind. What becomes of after?" Her glazed eyes would gaze out at the tree, and the boys, squatting together at her feet, would stare at their mother, transfixed, baffled, echoing her words, hoping to lace logic into her peculiar utterances.

It might have been these confusing afternoon sessions that created in the twins the odd habit of unconsciously echoing each other's words. It could also have been the fact that all during her pregnancy Mama Hayat had softly repeated to herself, "One becomes two. Two makes one." She would mutter this as her hands tapped a waltz across her tightening stomach drum, a distended dance floor for her fingers. Who knows what floating eggs hear or what effect the outside has on the in, but a mother's whispers, her incessant tapping, probably shape in unforeseeable ways. For twins, already uncommon, bagged together as they are, closer than close but with different fingerprints, the likelihood of an unusual outcome is no doubt doubled. Whatever the reason, Mish'al and Mishari made statements always together, never separately. When they spoke, they sounded as if they were sitting atop a great, craggy cliff in Wadi Ram. The volume of their voices would decrease as the repeated portion of their statement or question shortened. A conversation with their mother might have gone something like this, with one of them starting and the echo bouncing back and forth between them:

33

"Mama, could we please have eggs for breakfast?"

"eggs for breakfast?"

"for breakfast?"

"breakfast?"

"fast?"

"st?"

"Not today boys," Mama Hayat might have answered.

"But Mama!" Mish'al would begin.

"Mama!"

"ama!"

"ma!"

"a!"

"Why not?" Mishari would complete.

"not?"

"ot?"

"t?"

"Because it's blisteringly hot out. If you eat eggs on a day as hot as today, chickens will grow inside your bellies and, soon enough, you'll be laying your very own eggs to eat. Two little egg boys you will become, round as cherries and unhappy as plums. Now, useful as two egg-laying sons would be to me, is that something you could live with for the rest of your long lives?"

"No, Mama, not especially."

"ot especially."

"ecially."

"ally."

"y."

"No. I didn't think so. For lunch you'll be having chicken stuffed with fruitcake. For now, I'll put extra sugar in your milk and tea."

34

Mama Hayat never seemed to notice her sons' echoed speech. Maybe it was because they were born to her this way, their earliest gurgles and babbles already ricocheting between them. In a vacuum, oddities instantly lose their oddness, idiosyncrasies are registered as normal. Mish'al and Mishari spoke as one and their mother heard them as one. "One becomes two. Two makes one." She believed this, had perhaps even made it so, and she lived with the sound of her boys' voices harmonized inside her head. But when the boys left the vacuum of their small home, venturing beyond the mud brick paradise of their first eight years, the world outside was less oblivious. Pearl divers peering over the sides of their great, hand-built dhows, fishermen with shrimp-kissed baskets, gold-faced women selling henna from Oman and matches from Sweden in the covered *souk*, men sipping tea and gossiping together after *maghreb* prayer on the benches along the outside walls of the numerous *diwaniya*s along the shore – all were awestruck by what they heard, flummoxed by the flying trapeze act in language the twins performed without effort, without even, it seemed, awareness.

Uncanny repetitions generate discomfort. On seeing the boys striding through the streets in their clean, white *dishdasha*s, men and women alike would blink hard or rub their eyes with their knuckles to remind themselves that they weren't, in fact, seeing double but that Hayat's boys were just out again. It could be that because nobody in town had seen the twins until the boys were eight, they simply had not had the time to grow accustomed to their doppelgänger effect gradually. Or, perhaps, the first shock of seeing little yellow-haired, fair-skinned doubles walking down the narrow, shaded lane one unusually cool October day in 1946 had simply been too much for the town to get over, so that even ten long years later, at eighteen, the boys still left behind them a wake of shaky *bismillah*s and *a'uthubillah*s wherever they went. It was also possible that the real reason behind the perpetual unease felt by the townspeople whenever they caught glimpses of the twins was that it forced them to remember something cutting and nasty about themselves, something they collectively felt would be best forgotten. And on top of it all, when the people heard the twins' strangely echoing speech, it took everything in their power not to reach immediately for a leather strap or slipper to knock two forcibly back into one, to pound to dust the jarring effect of having to face their own shame, not once but twice.

Mama Hayat had sworn to herself she would cloister her boys only until they asked to see the world beyond their walls. She was grateful for the eight years. She had expected five, six at most. Some may judge cruel the decision to keep children locked up, preventing them from playing with kids their own age, from exploring the edges of their town and discovering their own versions of adventure. But Mama Hayat knew from experience that cruelty lurked outside her walls, not within them and not within her. She worked hard to transform their home into a place where enchantment was possible for her sons. She embroidered a world of words for Mish'al and Mishari. Her stories were threads of gold around their necks, her poems pearls tightly tucked in their closed fists. She sang old sea shanties to put them to sleep, her voice lilting through the house with the wind. Even her recipes transformed the

36

bland, repetitive ingredients available to her into lush, intricate meals it often took the boys days to figure out. Guessing ingredients was one of the games they would play with their mother while she sipped *istikan*s of tea, filling the time after lunch and before siesta.

"Fish, rice, and cardamom?"

"ice and cardamom?"

"ardamom?"

"mom?"

"Not fish. Not rice. Not cardamom."

"Wheat, chicken, cumin, and coffee?"

"cumin and coffee?"

"and coffee?"

"offee?"

"ee?"

"Coffee, yes. Wheat, chicken, and cumin, no."

Until their mother's lids would begin to droop, slow as melted sugar, the boys would shoot out as many combinations as they could, hoping to hit the mark.

In this way, Mama Hayat kept her sons curious and smart. She taught them to read, and they spent hours every day poring over the Qur'an. They also read chunks of novels, poems, and articles about places, people, and objects they had never heard of, in pages left at the foot of their mattress once a week. They didn't ask their mother how the stacks of ripped and crinkled pages got there. There was no one other than Mama Hayat; it had to be her. Still, they liked to keep open a crack of mystery, a flicker of someone (their father?) or something (the roots of their tree?) sneaking up into their room at night, leaving piles of mysterious paper clues for them to pore over. One thing years of isolation had produced in the twins was a leaping imagination. This, as they would learn once they left the protective walls of their little *kout*, or fortress, was rare in Kuwait and gave the townsfolk yet another reason to mistrust Hayat's unusual offspring.

Mish'al and Mishari learned instinctively, as children do, never to question their mother about their father. They tried to solve the riddle of their conception through traces they felt were everywhere to be found – in their mother's post-siesta murmurs, in her poems and stories, even the funny ones, in her food, in the pages left at the foot of their bed, in every corner of their safe home. They had not asked to creep out into the world because they had always figured it was the world inside that held the answers. Mama Hayat made them feel that way, and for the longest time they hadn't even real-ized a world outside their walls existed. When they were four or five, they began to notice that late in the evenings their mother would fold her layers of sleep dress around her body and steal down the stairs. They would hear the unfamiliar cluck of the heavy padlock, the creak of the lazy front door, and the sound of their mother whispering urgently to some-one whispering back. They did not, at this juncture, begin to prod Mama Hayat about letting them out. But they did begin to ask indirect questions about the padlock, the voices of neighbors, the steady arrival of supplies. They knew about fathers from their mother's stories and their own reading, and they would wonder about the invisibility of their own.

Hayat's story was not a complicated one. It had to do with an illicit relationship and the crossing of unmarked but widely

38

recognized lines in the sand. The blond hair that covered the round heads of her boys was not a result of albinism. Their hair was fair because somewhere in their genetic tangle, blond was strong. In 1937, the year Hayat met the father of her boys, Kuwait was overrun with oil diggers, many of them blond and British. Though they would set up camp in the desert and stay mainly out there, sometimes they would come down to the water's edge to coax the dust from underneath their nails, from between their knotted strands of hair. They would saunter into town, into the *souk*s, to remind themselves of chatter and bustle, to purchase coveted tobacco and kerosene, black ointment for boils, pomade to keep their hair in place. Kuwait was a port, a fishing and pearling town. The menfolk were regularly at sea, gone for months at a time, so the womenfolk often found themselves without male guardians. They took advantage of their autonomy by going out to select on their own the freshest flapping fish on the market, the longest grains of rice, the prettiest patterned cloth. Some of the women – widows, grandmothers, those with insistent mouths to feed – even started to sell everyday essentials themselves, displaying their wares on small square mats on the ground of what would come to be known as *Souk al-Hareem*, the women's *souk*. Kuwaiti women were used to dealing with traders arriving from Oman and India, and they were not shy about negotiating bargains. White men in search of scissors, thread, nails, locks, or matches would come to *Souk al-Hareem* to pick up what they needed and to stare curiously at the women covered in black selling to them, searching out their heavily kohled eyes. They were startled when these women stared back, when girlish giggles erupted from under the black cloth, when they felt themselves, incredibly, being flirted with. The women of Kuwait were headstrong. Staying within the confines of their closely built homes was out of the question.

Hayat was one of the *Souk al-Hareem* vendors. She had grown up an orphan. She may as well have grown up a prostitute or the daughter of a prostitute. Like twins and the mentally unstable, orphans were not well regarded in old Kuwait, and orphan girls were especially suspect. Orphans were viewed as rivals, trouble-makers, takers with nothing to give. They were at best snubbed or scorned, at worst beaten or otherwise abused. The difference between Hayat and the sorry lot of parentless children she grew up with in a dilapidated building at the edge of town was that she owned property and had a good bundle of money set aside, and everyone knew it. Since her land and her money were held in safekeeping by the town *mullah*, an old and honest friend of Hayat's father, nobody could weasel it away from her, though many tried. Like Hayat herself, Hayat's parents had been only children. The two had been unnaturally close, had loved each other ferociously, so the rumors went, and, one orange afternoon, had floated out to sea together on a small boat never to return. Their bodies had not washed up on shore, and none of the many ships passing in the area had sighted the lost vessel. Hayat, at four, had found herself very suddenly alone, without parents, grandparents, aunts, uncles, or cousins, without a friend in the world.

As far as Hayat was concerned, her childhood was sealed, off-limits, unmentionable. Nobody in town ever spoke to her of her vanished parents, and she never spoke to them of her dismal early years. At eighteen, when she moved into her home, the home that had once belonged to her father, and collected her inheritance from the old *mullah*, she decided the best way to proceed was discreetly. She quietly hired able hands to work for her – whitewashers, tilers, carpenters aplenty – but she did not open her doors to the neighborhood women or the gossips, not to the pious or the well-meaning or the simply curious. She wanted the bridge to the outside, to alliances of camaraderie especially, burned forever. Hayat's easy confidence was enough to repel would-be companions anyway. Her flagrant independence, deemed a threat, promptly became a source of acute envy. She walked through the streets with wide strides, routinely leaving behind the customary black cloth or gold *burka* so she could raise her pretty cheeks to the sun. No father, brother, uncle, or husband was around to tell her that such a thing simply was not done. She walked directly to wherever she wanted to go, never stopping along the way to visit with inquisitive neighbors. The townsfolk wondered whether anyone would ever stoop so low as to marry the brazen orphan girl. Wives, worried their husbands might be tempted to take Hayat on as a second, filled their ears with tales of her unruliness, her wayward conduct, never suspecting their words inflamed rather than dampened desire.

But Hayat wasn't there for the taking. She had made the decision never to marry. Late at night, she would sneak out of her house, walk to an isolated scrap of shore, and plunge into the forgiving warmth of the Gulf. Some nights, when the moon was absent, she even dared to swim without clothes. She knew marriage would mean giving up midnight swims and cheeks to the sun, that it would restrict the space she needed to stretch her toes, and she knew it couldn't possibly

41

be worth it. So Hayat sold her wares at the *souk*, tended her flowers, combined her far-flung ingredients, and bided her time.

Hayat never realized she was waiting for Iskandar, Iskandar and her echo twins. On one of his visits to the town center, he passed through *Souk al-Hareem*, looking over the displayed items, trying to collect everything he might need to survive the next month in the unforgiving desert. At Hayat's mat, he stalled: in a sea of black, her exposed face stood out like a beacon. He stared down at her in open astonishment. These were the first pair of female Kuwaiti eyes he had seen attached to a nose, a mouth, a chin, and cheeks. He squatted down fast and leaned in closer than he knew was advisable. Hayat remained still. He stabbed two of his fingers into the center of his chest.

"Alexander. Alexander."

Hayat said not a word. She stared back at him with quizzical, not unfriendly eyes.

"My name is Alexander. Your name? What ... is ... your ... name? *Ismek?*"

Hayat didn't answer. He noticed her look up from his aquamarine eyes to the flaxen hair on his head. He was accustomed to fascination over his hair. Men he worked with would often reach forward to touch it, sometimes even pulling out a strand or two to show their children. Hayat seemed to marvel, too, though she remained silent. Alexander gathered a few necessities off her mat, overpaid, and refused the change. Hayat stood up and shook her head at him violently, her black *abaya* cascading around her shoulders. She pushed the change firmly into his fingers, her hand slipping into his.

42

She said, "Hayat."

Alexander knew the women of the *souk* would begin to make their way home around noon, so he waited for Hayat outside the covered market. He saw her walk out from under the thatched awning, her face lifted, her gait strong. He followed her through the narrow streets, shadowless in the mid-afternoon sun, not hiding, but not making himself obvious either. Her house was on the edge of the sea, its outer walls splashed with bright blooms of bougainvillea. As she pulled open the heavy wooden front door, she turned to look back at this unusual Alexander, daring to follow an Arab woman in the streets, daring to stop in front of her home, daring to look her in the face, as if expecting something. She walked over the raised threshold and left the door ajar, daring Alexander a little further.

And why not? She was a young woman, no different from young women anywhere else. Her propriety had not been respected, growing up in that rotten home for orphans where much unpleasantness had occurred. Now, she wanted this foreign Alexander, hair the color of the lightest sand along the shore, sand she curled between her toes in the middle of the night. She would not respect propriety. Why should she? She was the orphan girl of parents who had loved with abandon, abandoned by them, as ready as they were to abandon this little fortress on the brink of thick, black disaster. Alexander was unearthing disaster in a desert that wasn't his. He dared to do it, foolishly oblivious. He dared to cross the threshold, stepping through to the other side, into her flowered isolation, Hayat's discreet life.

That night and for one night a month over the next six months, Hayat and Alexander slept together on the terrace.

43

Had anyone been looking, they would have glimpsed flashes of glacial white together with lean lengths of olive. Had anyone been peering over windowless walls and into private courtyards, they would have seen weaves of gold and black swelling over teak benches. Had anyone been listening, they would have heard echoes:

"Two makes one."

"Two makes one."

"Two makes one."

"Two makes one."

When she communicated to him, with moving hands and shimmering sounds, that Hayat meant life, he started calling her that. She called him "Iskandar," the Arabic version of Alexander.

"Iskandar Dhul-Qarnayn."

"Iskandar Dhul-Qarnayn."

"Iskandar Dhul-Qarnayn."

"Iskandar Dhul-Qarnayn."

Two-horned Alexander the Great. Hayat of the hanging gardens. Iskandar and Life, renamed, dazzled for seven nights. Had anyone been sniffing around, they would have smelled salty air, a spiced breeze, and longing in the curve of a white shell he brought in from the beach. At first, no one was there to see, to hear, to smell. No one suspected the rustling behind the fuchsia blooms, behind the cluck of her locking door. In quiet crevices, life is born over and over again, without witness, without recognition. It happens, feverishly or serenely, fast or slow, and the guardians of propriety remain laughably ignorant. But eventually, inevitably, they become aware, their fury rises, and they smash down hard, with an iron fist.

44

As the sixth month opened, Hayat began to show through her carefully arranged layers. Swift as the wind, the murder of crows gathered in close, circling with wet anticipation. After his seventh visit, as he stepped over the raised threshold and into the lavender light of predawn, Alexander was seized firmly by the arms and escorted to an alley close by, not out of view. He was placed gently onto the dusty ground, like a child into a cradle. He was kicked solidly three times in the ribs and twice in the groin. He was smacked on the side of the head and punched in both of his eyes and in the jaw. A stream of saliva, blood, and teeth seeped through his swollen lips. They rubbed mud into his straw hair and over his hot white skin. They spat on him once, twice, three times, as they turned on their heels and left him writhing. He crawled to the edge of town, back into the drilled desert, passing on his way the haunted building of Hayat's childhood (she had spoken to him of it in agonizing detail, in a language of tears), whispering gravely:

"One becomes two. One becomes two. One becomes two. One becomes two."

They had scared him, asserted their irrefutable ownership.

The townsfolk never approached Hayat directly, never threatened or harmed her in any way. She was left alone, her defiance sucked out as thoroughly as marrow from the bones of goats. Or so they chose to believe. Her front door locked, her walls a shield against them all, Hayat became invisible to the town. Apart from a sullen old acquaintance of the mats who willingly snuck supplies to her in the middle of the night, Hayat was not seen for eight years. After that, when the twins began to visit the world outside, only snatches of her would come into view through the door. They had broken the spell of those six months, her affair with Iskandar, fair-haired father of her boys. They had tried to stake their claim on her, just as the world outside, including Alexander, was staking its claim on the poison coursing through the veins of their land. But, to their surprise, Hayat slipped through. She banished them. They were left panting with curiosity about her life behind the walls, about her pregnancy – had it come to term? was it a boy or a girl? what was it called? – and about her plans for the future. They wondered what she thought of them, whether she understood what they had done, or whether she looked down on them with disdain. They were troubled to find they cared about her opinion, more and more as the years passed. From behind those walls, she, unlikely orphan girl, became their touchstone, their measure of cruelty and kindness, and they were ashamed of themselves, irredeemably ashamed of what they had done.

Hayat never learned exactly what had happened to Iskandar, and she never tried to find out. A week after their final encounter, she discovered a small tin box wrapped in white muslin carefully placed on her doorstep. It was heavier than it looked, a weight that sat comfortably in the palm of her right hand. With her fingers around that box came the certainty, the absolute certainty, that she would never see Iskandar again. She never did.

"Mama? What's in the box?"

"in the box?"

"the box?"

"box?"

"ox?"

This question was as close to a direct inquiry about their father as the boys would ever venture. It was a question they asked every night, repeated like a prayer or history. Mama Hayat had shown the twins the box on the morning they asked to go outside. She gathered her eight-year-olds into her arms, breathing in the smell of her womb, recognizing in their request the end of safety, the end of shelter, the end of living their enchanted ostrich lives. She felt already the obliteration of mud brick homes, of unbroken shorelines and crystal waters, of memory and a time before. It would all fall so quickly, and not just for her. So many ghosts to come. She could feel herself melting into an apparition. She could already see money exchanging hands for land. Hayat envisioned a desert partitioned, cordoned, flashing with flames of orange and red in the dead of night. She pictured the place little *Kout* would become and tried to imagine her boys in the middle of it. It made her fearful. She could no longer imagine herself there. She thought of Iskandar's box. Abruptly, Hayat released her hold on Mish'al and Mishari, both a little confused by their mother's show of desperate affection, and went to retrieve it.

"*Habaybi*, this box is your father's legacy. Inside it you will find your birthright. When I die, it belongs to you. For now, it belongs to me."

"Mama? What's in the box?"

"in the box?"

"the box?"

"box?"

"ox?"

Hayat kneeled down to face her boys, to look into their

47

eyes as deeply as she possibly could, to let them know that what she was going to say now, she would never say again.

"Mish'al and Mishari, my yellow-haired angels, inside this box is the answer to everything on earth. Inside is the end of war, the end of greed, the end of judgment, the end of jealousy, the end of selfishness, and, most importantly, the end of cruelty. But you have to wait until I'm dead to look. In the meantime, you must try to figure it out for yourselves. Go outside these walls, past the edge of this town, deep into the desert. Talk to as many people as you can. Ask questions. Take notes. And when you come home, start sorting, start piecing, start weaving. I can't help you any longer. You're on your own for now. Courage. Courage."

Though they asked Mama Hayat the same question every night, hoping to trick her into revealing some tiny clue, she never said another word about it. Her only response to their nightly inquiry was, "Goodnight, my flaxen ropes. I love you forever and a day away from everything we think we know and love."

"Goodnight Mama. We love you back."

"ama. We love you back."

"ove you back."

"ou back."

"ack."

As her boys plunged into the world beyond her borders, Hayat felt, for the first time in years, alone. She was confident they would swim through their new life, her defiant gait as embedded in their genetic code as their father's blond hair. In the space they left behind, she came to miss Iskandar, or something Iskandar might have become had he been given the chance. She began to dream of his closed eyes, lashes like flecks of gold on his cheeks. While the boys were out, she started to spend more time with the tin box, carefully unfolding the muslin, unlocking the small clasp, removing the familiar object from inside. It was the feeling of floating in the warm fold of the sea, naked with the crabs and the shrimps and the groupers. Hayat would sit under her *sidr* tree, the singing of sparrows and bulbuls in her ears, the bluest of skies in her eyes, the lovely weight of Iskandar's gift in her hands, and she would feel time collapse into something other than it happened to be at that moment. She would drift outside the lines in the sand, toward a glow around something she could almost make out, was on the verge of seeing clearly. It was like galloping through water or shooting up into the sun. Almost past the limit, just about there, pushing against the pull of her boys, their whorl of love echoing in her soul. But Hayat could not surrender, could not ascend toward that orb, that promise left behind. She would wrap up Iskandar's legacy, hide it where she knew the boys would never look, and spend the rest of the morning, the rest of her days, whistling with the wind, cooking treats for her twins.

The town the boys emerged into, stepping over their mother's threshold for the first time, was a town on the brink. The Alexanders of Arabia had found what they had come to find. By 1946, oil was vatted and ready to launch across seas and oceans accustomed, for hundreds of years, to carrying spices, jewels, textiles, water. Everyone around was touting change, splendor, and the end of misery. Money, unprecedented, would soon cascade, and the demolition of history would begin. Arched corridors, hidden courtyards, and shared terraces no more. After the initial shock of encountering the twins for the first time, the townsfolk tolerated their presence. Though they would never gather them warmly into fat, welcoming arms, the coincidence of dates caused the people of old Kuwait to interpret the startling appearance of the twins as a sign of miracles to come. Mish'al and Mishari's blond heads, viewed bobbing through the narrow alleys or in the waters of the Gulf or around the dhow yards, their three favorite places to be, were considered early on as sigils of good fortune.

But with time, the boys began to generate more unease than comfort. Strange doubled beings and odd echoed speech soon came to symbolize to the increasingly bewildered residents the Janus-faced reality of producing and exporting oil. The mad fantasy of riches would come, but it would come on a wave of seismic destruction. Long after the echo twins were wafers in the memory of only the oldest Kuwaitis, the destruction still rained down, harder and harder. Crystal waters no more. Bluest skies no more. Delicate white truffles bursting in the desert no more. *Sidr* trees no more. Razed and replaced. Out with the old. To this day nobody knows for certain what has come instead. In with some vicious, damaging thing. In with perplexity. In with loss.

The boys, following their mother's instructions, spent the years of their youth talking to the townsfolk, asking them questions, writing down the details they didn't want to forget. Mish'al and Mishari collected snippets of their mother's life: an orphan with an inheritance, parents lost at sea, obstinate girl with face uncovered, cheeks raised to the sun. Some

50

mentioned that, like the twins, their mother had once loved to swim; it was, after all, no secret. Most kept their mouths shut about the twins' father. But a few, only one or two really, mentioned digging in the desert and Britannia. They let slip blond hair and the night. They brought up love. Nobody ever said anything about the end, but Mish'al and Mishari, made clever by the clues their mother had taught them to read throughout their childhood, put two and two more or less together.

"One becomes two."

"becomes two."

"omes two."

"s two."

"wo."

The twins echoed their mother's story as they wandered around the narrow lanes of old Kuwait, as they swam through the waters of their sea, as they swung from the timber skeletons of dhows under construction. Back and forth to each other, building up stories about Mama Hayat, about their father, about themselves, and then, increasingly, about the people they lived among. They fashioned tales, wild and roaming, unhampered by facts. They imagined away the restrictions of place. They created in leaps that hopped across time. They felt free, taking in long, deep breaths as they built for themselves a home in language, a shelter they carried everywhere with them, turning the heads of those who caught fragments of their oral symphony.

But the twins never once forgot about the box. It contained, they were certain, the answer to every question they ever had. Their mother had said so. Their mother was dead. She never revealed to them where the box was hidden, but they knew. It could only be in one place.

Mish'al and Mishari washed their mother's body and wrapped her in white linens, preparing her for the next morning, her journey into the desert. They could not bear to think of Hayat's body abandoned in the sands now drilled with holes, safety there no more. They placed an unnecessary pillow under her covered head and left her lying on the mattress they had so often pulled out together onto the terrace. Later that evening, the feel of their mother's weight still in their arms, the twins descended to the courtyard, sat on one of the benches, and stared at the familiar tree, old enemy, old friend. It was there, they knew, hidden somewhere under the tangle of roots. It was time to open the box.

At midnight, in the white light of a moon turning waves into plains of snow, the twins carefully unwrapped their legacy. The muslin, brown from years of wind storms and rain, disintegrated to dust between their fingers. The tin was rusted, the lock no longer locked. The brothers caught their breath as they removed from the box a heavy object not immediately clear in the shadows along the shore. Mish'al held it up to the moon.

"A compass."

"compass."

"pass."

"ss."

A heavy brass-cased compass. F. Barker & Son. Trade Mark London. Sharp black points in all directions: north, south, east, west, northeast, southeast, northwest, southwest, and twenty-four others in between. Black on white dial. A heavy little orb with glass catching the twinkling stars and the lunar light as Mish'al and Mishari passed it back and forth to each other with mounting pleasure. The world resting unexpectedly in their palms. A removable brass lid was engraved with the initials: ASK. The brothers held Alexander between them. Their mother's Iskandar Dhul-Qarnayn, her two-horned lover, their father. Hayat's version of life pointed them now in a direction they had not foreseen.

"Time to go," whispered Mishari.

"Yes," Mish'al concurred.

III

An odd and inexplicable flash of light. Where was it coming from? Sitting at the bottom of the stairs, I tried to peer into the darkness at the top.

"Isn't it strange how that keeps happening?"

"What does?"

"That flash. Every once in a while I see a flash."

"I hadn't noticed."

I wasn't surprised he hadn't noticed. All he could think about was that some girl, the love of his life no less, had broken up with him. This compact, earnest boy had recently moved to the American School of Kuwait, ASK. I don't know how we became friends – the only Kuwaiti boy I would ever befriend and not for long – but my patience over his misfortune was fast running out. Even here, at this remarkable party (and it really was astonishing: a villa empty of furniture, police bouncers at the door, a bar on every floor), all he could do was go on and on about the pain, the ache, the sorrow. I wanted to stuff his broken heart with a bouquet of pink carnations.

At the end of the year, I would add to the hurt of his heart a bit myself, would go with him to a dance – as his friend, that was the agreement – and then leave him for Jonas. This little gentleman would soon be angry with me. But that was still months and months away, forever in adolescent time.

"Look, I'm going inside to dance for a while. Coming?"

"You go ahead. I think I'll stay out here."

He stood as I stood – was he ever polite – then sat back down and lit another cigarette. I didn't see him again that night. I couldn't understand the extent of his sorrow over a girl. It felt sticky, unseemly for a boy already sixteen. I was trying hard to be nice to the new guy, but I couldn't be around it all for too long. It felt like waking up smothered by sheets hiked over your chest. It felt like clenched fists.

Walking into the tar black room at the top of the stairs was a wide stretch of relief. The place was nothing – a black box with blacked-out windows, dark and moist, with kids leaning against walls. The place was everything. I wandered into the middle of it, into the dancing center, crowded bodies parting for a split second to let me in. Hands thrust up, pushing high, torsos swaying, determined, and, suddenly, strange arms catching me. "Holy girl your lips of clay." Someone's liquid breath against my neck. Again, that flash – in it, chandelier crystals floated above us then disappeared. I threw my head back and fell into the music, into alien arms. "Will whisper words of yesterday." I was outside the new boy's heartache. I was free. I would guard against his wall of lost potential. His weariness would not be mine. "Absolute a principle to make your heart invincible." I would dance in the black box forever, my arms waving, my hips gliding – watch me.

Another flash and there he was, leaning against the wall, white kerchief knotted around his neck. "A girl to make a dream come true." I saw Jonas see me.

~

The

Diary

It hadn't started out as a diary. It began as a log of quietly observed and methodically recorded details.

Monday, June 16, 1980. Rip in black trash bag. Smells very bad. Sticky trail left along sidewalk. Small birds whispering outside window. Yellow skies in afternoon before storm. Bright lightening comes after cracking thunder. Fish fingers are not always crispy.

For a while, it was page after page of carefully chronicled minutiae. Mina carried the notebook – made in China, black with red triangle corners and binding – everywhere. At the unlikeliest moment, before going down a slide, seconds after the lights dimmed in a movie theater, the instant she blew out her birthday candles, she would flip it open, write something down, slam it shut again.

Wednesday, March 11, 1981. Mirrors reflect light and eggplants do too. Smoke rises even as hot wax sinks.

Marbles get dusty when played with. Sometimes the sun hangs pink and low. Cages can't trap light.

Her father found his daughter's habit disconcerting and intriguing. Her mother was initially encouraging, then mildly curious, but as time passed, increasingly uneasy.

The first-person pronoun changed everything. Two years after she first began to write in the notebooks, Mina, with her cropped fringe and slow-blinking eyes, discovered that describing objects wasn't the only thing words could do. Her words, initially shy, were now more boldly wrapping themselves around her and other people.

Saturday, September 25, 1982. He doesn't always wipe his mouth with the napkin his mother packs in his lunch. Sometimes he trades his plain milk for chocolate. When he raises his left hand to answer a question, he rests his right hand over his heart, like Napoleon. I wonder if he knows I watch him and that I carry him home with me after school.

Language was slinking into smooth, dark corners, places with sharp crevices oozing disorder. She worked her way through the jumble, slow at times, other times quick.

Tuesday, February 7, 1984. I continue to obsess over the things others remember. We all carry little packets of memories. Some of us put our packets into little boxes. Some of our boxes have keys that are sometimes worn on a leather cord around the neck, sometimes kept in a bank security box opened with yet another key, sometimes plunked in a drawer of trinkets and trash. Some of us keep our packets on shelves, others in closets. I have a suspicion that our packets are actually all laced together so that if any are dropped or misplaced or buried, it won't be forever. Though there is no guarantee they will return to the original holder. I am constantly tripping over dropped packets and lost keys.

Notebooks, always made in China, always smelling of an apothecary shop in Beijing or Shanghai, were filled at an extraordinary rate. By the time Mina turned fourteen, the diary was her second skin, her life lived twice.

That year, a teacher gave Mina books to read, other people's writing. He noticed her in a classroom of forty kids, mostly because she hadn't noticed him. He was too old for her to notice. He tried to convince himself that it didn't really matter. It didn't matter, he told himself, that she smelled of sea salt. It didn't matter that she bit her lower lip when she stared unnervingly, never at him, with his horn-rimmed glasses, tan slacks, checked shirts, and moustache. It didn't matter that she still hadn't quite learned how to arrange her legs under the navy blue skirt of her uniform. It didn't matter that her eyes, when the sun hit them, were brown and not the olive-stone black they appeared indoors. What mattered to him ultimately, desperately, was that the potential he saw coiled tight in her, as tight as the knot in his own stomach whenever she passed his room, had to be released. He could not leave it to her parents. How could they possibly see the future of this child they had conceived? Parents cling to their children's pasts; they belong to them. Most cannot fathom that their children's yet-to-comes will never be theirs. They grasp with gentle tentacles, drowning their oblivious offspring in love or guilt. Against these parental impulses, against his better judgment, he started to unravel Mina's coil, bit by bit. He selected authors for her to read: Kafka, Woolf, Durrell, Márquez, Kundera. She carefully read each one, curled up on the small landing of the carpeted stairs at home, her skin warmed by slants of afternoon sun.

She had been reading her whole life, so this was nothing new. Her mother, who had inherited the obsessive reading gene from her father, had read tirelessly to her improbably alert baby, everything from Mother Goose to Dr. Seuss. When her grandfather died, her mother had given Mina one of his books, a first edition of *The Wizard of Oz*. Mina could smell her grandfather's life in the pages of that old book, which had found its unlikely desert home only because, in his youth, a curious Arab man had become captivated by the story of a childhood that could never have been his own. In it she smelled pipe smoke and cigarettes, whiskey and gripe water. She smelled the dust of his old projector which had worn out reels and reels of Laurel and Hardy, whom he preferred, only slightly, over the Marx Brothers. She smelled his overfull but fully ordered bedroom, its cool gray marble floors and heavy velvet curtains pulled almost completely shut, allowing only the slightest splinter of daylight to prick in and illuminate the suspended dust. She smelled his big creaky bed, quilted with neat piles of paper, and even the plastic of the ivory Ericofon he was so proud of, its dial hidden from sight. She smelled her mother's childhood in Pune, layers of mango ice cream, sliced papaya, and jackfruit.

The pages of that old book were heavy with her grand-father's losses. His small trading company in India had gone bankrupt, and during the sad voyage back to Kuwait, he had lost his restless audacity too. The desert had never been to his liking and working for the national oil company – where, after all, it was only one thing everyone was after – had violated his sense of enterprise. His life became less about what he was doing or going to do and more about what he had already done. Every weekend, Mina and her cousins would flock to his quarters – a library, a bedroom, and the avocado green tiled bathroom where soon he would have his heart attack quickly and alone, the false teeth he used to frighten and delight the children still floating in a small glass beside the sink. He would recount to them how he had sailed off to India in a dhow, against the wishes of his parents, to look for rubies, sapphires, emeralds, and other glittering things. He would tell them how he had met their grandmother, where else but in a garden, under a banyan tree, and how her father, their great grandfather, had openly balked at the idea of his precious fairy daughter marrying an unreliable Arab jewel trader, however keenly intelligent and well-read. Love won the day, and soon many children were born.

"My mother?" Mina would always ask at this point.

"Indeed, your mother. My youngest and" – he would whis-per in an aside to his beloved granddaughter – "favorite. I had wanted to name her Mina but was not allowed to on the obstinate authority of your grandmother. So when you were born, Mina, I insisted that your mother give you the name I had chosen especially for her all those years ago. And she did, my darling daughter. So, here you are Mina, Mina, full of my dreams, full of my love." Those last words he would often chant to her playfully but also, she thought, with nostalgia. "Mina, Mina, full of my dreams, full of my love."

While Mina consumed books with hunger and without discrimination as a child, it was on the edge of young adulthood, with the books earnestly selected for her by a fawning teacher, that words began to seep into her living moments. Sometimes there was confusion.

Tuesday, January 1, 1985. I must create a life to look back on, a life I can search for in the future, time now that will inevitably be lost only to be found once again. I must live my life then write about it. Or maybe I should write my life then live it.

Like her grandfather before her, Mina felt the restless urgency to move, the longing for travel. But Mina was much younger than her grandfather had been when he sailed away romantically on a handmade dhow in search of adventure. Plus, she was not an Arab man but an Arab girl, and trouble was inescapably enfolded in the pages of her wayward desires.

It was the year of the carefully selected books that Mina began to craft encounters. One morning in winter, she jumped out of her bedroom window and hitched a ride to the sea in the truck of a mildly shocked but mostly amused Bedouin man. He told her that his own three daughters were never out of his sight and wouldn't dream of being in a car with a stranger.

"But they're out of your sight now."

"Yes, but their mother is with them."

"What if she isn't?"

"She must be."

"But she's out of your sight too."

"Yes, but I can see her in my mind's eye."

"But can that eye really see?"

"It sees what's important." She gave him the last word but he seemed less amused. Mina noticed that he had a sharp frown crease cutting into his brow. She had made him uneasy. He dropped her off where she asked, mumbled something unintelligible, and drove off. The rocks where she sat were warmer and lonelier than she had expected. She noted this in the diary.

Then there was the boy she would run with who kept a mysterious, small leather pouch in his pocket. She would wait for him to walk in through the school gates. He would see her, peripherally, but pretend he hadn't. He would normally arrive seconds before the bell rang; she wished he would come earlier. One afternoon, during lunch break, she ran and he gave chase. She flew into the boys' locker room. It was empty. She dashed into the showers and stopped. He bumped into her from behind, lifted her up, put her down again. They looked into each other's eyes.

"What's in the pouch?"

Instead of answering, he bit her arm hard, like he wanted to take a bite out of it. He ran out. She rubbed the spit left behind into her skin.

Later she invented reasons for why she had a bruise in the shape of teeth on her arm, one for each person who asked.

"I bit my own arm in my sleep because I had a toothache."

"My cousin has a monkey that bites the arms of girls who don't wear gingham dresses."

"An accident with a plunger."

Everything but what had really happened, which belonged, in part, to the diary.

Sometimes, instead of spending the night at her best friend's house as she had told her parents, she would skip off to one of the weekend parties thrown in inexplicably empty villas with designated floors for drinking and dancing, a policeman guarding the front door. Mina would try to take furtive photographs. She got the idea at a party once after noticing flashes that could have been lightening but were more likely something else. It was not risk-free to take pictures since, like her, many weren't supposed to be at these parties and certainly wanted no material evidence that proved otherwise. In the middle of dancing she would pull out her little camera, raise it above her head, aim it downwards, and snap phantom photos. Usually people were too drunk to register the sudden flash in the dark or, if they did, couldn't figure out what it was.

One night, Mina found herself on an undesignated floor. There didn't seem to be anyone around, unusual for these parties. The area was unlit, but it looked like an extremely narrow corridor led from the top of the stairs to an open door. Mina felt her way along the corridor. She began to hear a distinct scratching and clicking sound. At the end of the corridor, she poked her head through the door and made out a wide figure huddled in the dark, completely still but for her hands.

"Who are you?" Silence. Mina asked again in Arabic.

Though she was sitting only about a meter away, the old woman's voice echoed as if from across a wide valley. "I have to finish removing the stones from this rice. It must be ready in time."

"In time for what?"

"In time for lunch. The men will bring the fish. Fish out of water must be plunged immediately into pools of rice."

"But do you live here? Who are you?" Mina noticed that the scratching and clicking came from the woman's fingernails running across an empty tin plate. There was no rice in the plate and no discarded stones either. She took photos of the absences so she could write about them later.

Mina had always been fascinated by her grandmother's collection of birds. Her grandmother had only agreed to leave India to return with her husband to his Arabian land on the condition that she be permitted to bring along her birds, each and every one. If Mina's grandfather's quarters were clouded with suspended book and projector dust, her grandmother's quarters were strewn with floating bird feathers. Screaming greens and shiny blues, upbeat yellows and fancy pinks, Mina felt like she had stepped into a conjuror's box of tricks whenever she made her way through the room. Her grandmother spent her mornings in private, drinking tea, milky and sweet, and talking to the macaws, the mynas, the rose-ringed parakeets, the cockatoos, each in turn. Mina would listen through a small crack in the door. She would catch fragments of sentences in her grandmother's lilting voice. Did she hear her grandmother tell the birds that madness ran in the family like an ostrich through the savanna? Was that why she had decided

67

to escape India? Could the murmurs about her own children be true? Only in the pages of Mina's diary did her birdwoman grandmother take flight. As far as everyone else was concerned, she was a no-nonsense old lady who happened to like birds.

At first, Mina didn't realize she was crafting encounters, and even after it began to dawn on her, she wasn't quite sure why. It was only at the end of that year, when the boy with the pouch revealed its contents to her, that she began to understand. All along, she had been crafting encounters that would make good stories. Stories to keep you up all night reading them as they helped put you to sleep. Stories you wished would never end as they pushed you to finish. Stories that would leave holes in you even as they provided plugs. Stories for only some to believe and even them only sometimes. They were the kinds of stories Mina had been writing in the diary all year without realizing. The diary compulsion had become overpowering, impossible to fight. It wasn't just the absurd or atmospheric that would be recorded. Everything – every conversation, every experience, every thought, every feeling – was filtered through the diary lens. From the loss of religion to the loss of virginity, the diary was a testament to the life of a young girl living at cross-purposes with a crusty society. Mina was protected from the potential crush of its wrath only because she was discreet and because few could be bothered to investigate the incessant scribbling of a child. Though she was changing no faster than the desert landscape overrun by petrodollar construction, it was too fast for the self-appointed guardians of customs and traditions in whose name all manner of things were kept in check. Unless there was money to be made.

The diaries took over Mina's room. Notebooks and scraps of paper to be transferred into notebooks were stashed in every available corner. Under her bed, between her bed frame and mattress, behind her dresser, among the books on her bookshelves: diaries. This awkward stashing was her feeble attempt at secrecy. She told herself she didn't want anyone to read her words but would sometimes relish the thrill of imagining what it would be like if curiosity got the better of someone. What would they think about her narrow escapes, her hits and misses, her nows or nevers? She often wrote with imagined eyes hovering over her shoulders but registered those eyes as a dare rather than a threat. She could not predict that when the imagined happened, when hovering eyes landed, there would be no pleasure in it, no thrill, nothing but a vortex of shame and guilt.

It wasn't until two years later, at the end of a summer filled with clandestine car rides and music played late into the night in other people's rooms, that the first horror occurred. Mina came home one scorching afternoon to find her diaries in tidy piles all over her room. It was a New York City of notebooks, paper skyscrapers forming a grid across the floor. Her mother sat silently on the bed, Mina's most recent diary butterflied open on her lap. It would be too easy and not exactly accurate to describe the look on her mother's face as shock. It was more the look that follows shock. Her face was as still as a Himalayan mountain top, as if the nerves under her skin were no longer capable of accepting or responding to stimuli, her blood cells unable to advance single-file through her capillaries. Her mother did not move as Mina walked into the room, but her exhausted eyes looked into her daughter's, searching for something familiar.

"Are these words true? Are these terrible stories about my family true? Have you really done such reprehensible things?"

Mina found it impossible to slice her own silence with any plausible explanation. How, with the evidence set before them in its grid-like glory, could she explain that the truth could be stretched in more than one direction at once, that it wasn't for her to say whether or not the words that emerged out of her pen, the words she had never thought to restrain, contained such a thing as truth? If anything, the diaries had always been a place for the dissolution of truth, where the truth could be picked apart and left to reassemble differently than it did on the outside. But it wasn't Mina's place to explain such things. She accepted the guilt implied by her silence. She accepted the tears that her words had caused to stream down her mother's face as a judgment worse than any that could be meted out by an unforgiving and merciless God she didn't believe in anyway. Mina would never be able to put together her mother's broken face, at least not in her own mind's eye, an eye, as it turned out, as focused as the confident Bedouin had once claimed.

As far as Mina could see, the only solution was to burn everything. To burn every notebook, every piece of crumpled paper, every word on every scrap was the only way to rub out the betrayal and scrape the shame. Mina brought in large, black trash bags that smelled of petroleum, opened them wide, and started to layer the doomed lot one atop the other. There were exactly one hundred notebooks, all black, all with red corners and binding. She did not allow herself to think for too long about the contents of her one hundred notebooks. Her mind was like a huge desert moth with furry wings. With every downward flap, the unraveled coil in Mina curled tightly up inside her once again. This was the cost of betrayal, the price of atonement. If Mina had known that death would come anyway, sooner than either she or her mother ever would have believed, that survival could be stolen in a flash, would she still have burned the notebooks? Probably.

The ensuing bonfire was celebratory. The stinking smoke of plastic bags and raped language did little to diminish this festival of imagined rebirth. Mina invited her sad mother and bewildered father to join in the late night merriment. Her mother acknowledged the gesture with a gentle hug. Her father, oblivious of his wife's recent discoveries, wondered why this was happening. Nobody, not even Mina, could explain, and he quickly decided not to probe. The next morning, Mina could not get out of bed. Outwardly, her body registered a fever. Inwardly, it felt like her lungs and stomach had been scooped out. The violence of what she had done the night before hit her full force, and she didn't think she could survive the realization. She felt herself deflating, becoming smaller and smaller, as small as a tadpole in a rotten swimming pool. She whimpered all afternoon.

A tidy life was what Mina led after the big explosion of 1987. She continued to keep a diary but no longer crafted encounters or wrote stories. Her new notebooks contained mostly stolid accounts of the day-to-day, with hidden sparks. She invented a code so veiled only she could crack it, though not without fail. It was always possible that after a few years or hours she would lose the key. *Wednesday, April 19, 1989. Interesting class on Romantic poetry* could simply mean that she had enjoyed the class or that she had slept with the boy in the fourth row with the blazing gaze. *Tuesday, May 29, 1990.*

Vanquishing desire could mean that she was clamping down on the unpredictable little eruptions of yearning that would suddenly scramble the surface of her complacency or that she had had an especially enjoyable breakfast.

A few coded lines a year for over a decade, and then, the second horror, an event for which there could be no code.

Sunday, September 9, 2001. Mother dead meant that disease had wracked her mother's fading body for ten months, that tubes and machines had been intimately involved, and that she had slipped away forever one quiet afternoon in a medically induced sleep. Unequivocally.

Fifteen years after Mina's decision to burn her childhood, her adolescence, to burn, essentially, herself, regret began its steady throb. The diary flow had slowed to an irregular trickle. There was no need for words when once wide-open dreams were slamming shut like shop-fronts in the gold *souk* at midday prayer. Mina's coil of potential was now so tightly wound it was a knot inside her. The whirl of stories, half true, half something besides, stopped. She felt as futile as a mirage, all shimmer and no quench. She became what all children of promise and their teachers dread most: ordinary. Her life without words was as dull as stale cornflakes. But this she could have lived with because extraordinary events continued to happen even if nobody happened to write them down. What had become unbearable to her was not so much the absence of words present as the lament for words past.

The realization crept up innocently enough early one morning in her mother's bird garden. Unlike her grandmother's room, her mother's garden was not full of glamorous varieties. It attracted plain little sparrows that stopped to drink cool water from the terracotta dish hanging from the wide lacy branches of an old *sidr* tree. Her mother would thoughtfully fill the dish for them every morning at dawn. After her death, Mina continued to do the same, though, unlike her mother, she didn't especially enjoy waking up early. Sometimes she slept late, and on those days small panting birds were left thirsty for hours, blinking at each other in confusion from across a dry dish. However, on this particular morning, Mina had managed to wake early enough to avoid guilt over parched chirps. She provided cool water then stretched her bones out on the grass.

The sun was not yet overhead and it was breezy enough to forget that only two months earlier it would have been impossible to spend five minutes outside air-conditioned space. Mina was doing what people do when they have half an hour or so to kill before work or errands or taking care of responsibilities that once belonged to someone else. She was musing in random patches. Fidgety thoughts rested for a second or two before moving along. Her finger played casually with her bellybutton – that funny little cave which at one time linked her flesh so intimately to her mother's. A stray petal of bougainvillea landed on her exposed belly.

In Kuwait, bougainvillea is called *mejnooneh*, crazy, notably in the feminine. Crazy because the fuchsia tissues multiply with an exuberance bordering on madness despite the heat and dryness. That this unique form of insanity was marked feminine always appealed to Mina the diarist who, as a girl, imagined writing down her observations, her owlish insights, on hundreds, thousands, millions of crazy petals in gold ink and then releasing them into a sky as tragically blue as the Mediterranean. She pictured the massive cloud of pink tissue petals, gilded feathers without bird bodies to keep them together. She thought of the people who might glance up expecting to see nothing more exotic than a pigeon only to find a ball of fuchsia rustling overhead, low enough to reach up and grab. Each person would end up with a single petal. If they were lucky, it would be meaningful to them. If not, and they happened to be standing beside someone who had also grabbed at the impossible floating pinkness, an exchange could be arranged. For example, *It is sometimes unreasonable to expect the world to mirror your responses* could be traded for *Cacti that look like artichokes are wrapped blessings*. Or, *To be left alone in a lonely place means only that joy is invisible, not absent* might be swapped in favor of *Stairs may lead to nowhere and doors may open onto a steep drop*. The young Mina had filled pages and pages with her fragments, believing, with a degree of arrogance masquerading as largesse, that one day they would firework the desert skies as never before.

Mina tried to peel the *mejnooneh* petal off her belly with her thumb and forefinger, attempting, unsuccessfully, to keep it intact. It was crushed, leaving in its place the electric pink dust that memories are made of. Inhaling this memory dust was pleasant enough at first. Fuchsia tissue petals and gold ink, parrot feathers and mysterious pouches, recommended books and *The Wizard of Oz*. But it wasn't long before towering paper sky scrapers began to shadow the horizon and, worse still, to come tumbling down. Red triangle corners started to bleed into the white muslin of memories fluttering in her head. She felt the loss of each moment twice, first to flames, then to time. Mild discomfort turned into a gigantic concrete brick of anxiety lodged tightly in her throat. She couldn't swallow, but she ached to regurgitate the pages burned to ashes. What had she done? What had she done? She descended into a notebook-shaped hell of her own making. She was now in her thirties with a lost-and-gone-for-ever past and a future she couldn't put into words. She had shed her writing skin with such effervescent ease. Now she was paying a price that had not been disclosed up front. She didn't know how to sweep the ashes back to the place where words resided.

After the morning in the garden, the brick-in-the-throat panic would knock Mina out anywhere, any time of day or night. There were no special triggers after the petal of bougain-villea, though she got into the habit of reading the world as a basket of signs addressed especially to her. Without being aware of it – it had become an unconscious tic – she would go through the day trying to single out which sign would this time jolt her back to the years she could not rewrite. Which mark among many would fill her mouth with a cement taste she could not rinse out? Would it be that snag in her navy pleated skirt? That light sneaking through the keyhole? That chewed-up red pencil with the small plastic compass attached? That faded white box in the gutter melting a touch more every day? That folded paper boat with the finger smudges? That fish in the heavy silver tray? In her head she prepared compressed captions for the proliferating signs around her, which she registered as Polaroid shots:

75

Snag in navy blue
Sneaky light
Teeth-pocked pencil
Melting boxes
Folded boat
Fish

While the others remained in her head, this last one she wrote down thoughtfully in a slim notebook of cheap recycled paper she had recently bought at the supermarket. *Fish.*

And then curiously and without warning, after two years of caption lists and bricked-up breathing, after seventeen years of diary death, something more.

Wednesday, July 21, 2004. When my mother died, the fish in the sea committed collective suicide. Millions upon millions of broken fish washed up on shore and the entire country smelled of rotting corpses. It should have been a national emergency, but it wasn't. Private citizens responded in odd and quiet ways. Some walked along the silvered shoreline shaking their heads in dismay, mouths and noses sheathed with head scarves and hands. Others stayed home to avoid breathing the noxious air, as they had in the days of the burning wells. Public announcements declared that only the heads were poisonous but that all other fish flesh was healthy to consume. Fish head soup out; fried fish tails in. Newspaper experts objected to government claims but offered no explanations of their own. It didn't matter since there were neither heads nor tails of fish left in the sea to eat. People murmured jagged concern in private corners.

But mostly the population just got on with a life without fish. I, however, like a forgotten phantom at the end of a dark corridor, cannot get on with a life without fish. I mourn for them, for my mother, for the loss of my life in the present tense.

IV

Ice in the desert. Not in Switzerland or Germany or Wisconsin. Not in a place where lakes turn milky as waters slow in late autumn, then stop for a while. To walk into an ice rink in the full heat of the desert and to feel your cheeks rise pink is miraculous and makes you believe that anything, just about anything, is possible.

Every Wednesday, the last day of the school week, we would all meet at the rink in the early evening. Standing around outside before the doors opened, we would eye the competition from other schools and try to find out what was happening that weekend, where the party was going to be. At the rink: the best greasy fries in the world and Michael Jackson blaring, a star, a hero, and, we were convinced, Billie Jean's lover. At the rink: learning to lace up skates, learning that kissing involves wetness, tongues, time. At the rink: holding tingling hands with girls, with boys, with both if you wanted, knowing it was all right, Michael muffling the wail of mosques outside.

Alex would come to the ice rink to skate seriously. He played hockey on Sundays and Tuesdays. On Wednesdays, he would whizz through the rest of us, blades so sharp they sprayed a fan of snow when he stopped, hard and sudden. There's an Alex at every school – beautiful, athletic, smart. But the Alex at our school was also distant, like he was hiding something, which made him even more

79

wondrous in our eyes. We all worshipped Alex – German-Palestinian god – whose second cousin on his father's side would, in a few years, accidentally blow himself up in a garden. Alex was the girls' common denominator, our irresistible sorcerer. Kissing Alex at the rink – just that once – was kissing moonlit perfection. I was fourteen, maybe fifteen, and I lifted my chin up to meet Alex's lips. A throwaway kiss at the rink, like kissing glory. We hardly exchanged a word. We exchanged, instead, our youth in small, private packets. In that worn army jacket, he was, for an instant, mine. He smiled so rarely, tall, flawless Adonis, but that night – just that once – he smiled for me.

Years later, I heard from someone, I can't remember who, that Alex was damaged, somehow broken. It's very possible. Alex was, after all, too good for the universe to allow to be true for too long. That night at Elsa's, all I could do was jump up and down on her bed screaming, "I kissed Alex! I kissed Alex!" It could never, not ever, get better than Alex at the rink.

~

Playing

with

Bombs

Death is not what they promised. No one-way ticket to paradise. No special dispensation for martyrs. No *houri*s. Those *houri*s were supposed to be awesome. I looked all over for them after the blast. Nothing. Time seems to pass over here, though I'm not exactly sure how it moves. In the ways that count, I think I'm still fifteen.

I had friends who could identify every specimen of bomb. I would stand around rolling my eyes and gnawing into my cheek as they rattled off names, model numbers, and destructive capabilities. Some of them sat around all day making lists like the ones kids in normal places make of their favorite athletes or rock stars. I was surprised they didn't hide posters of artillery under their pillows in place of *Playboy* centerfolds. My best friend Rami had photocopies of *Playboy* pictures hidden under his bed, and, God forgive us, they were fantastic.

I, on the other hand, couldn't have cared less about explosives. I hated what they did and never got angry enough to want to use them, not even against our sworn enemies. That made me different – a loner, an outsider, on the fringe. Oh, and I loved that. I was fifteen and reading Camus and Dostoevsky, what do you want from me? A couple of years earlier, there was the *intifada*. That was a dynamite moment, and I was as fired up as all my friends were. Everyone who knew me made fun of the fact that at last something had yanked me out of my corner and into the streets. "From books to stones, eh, Nimr? This is what it takes to get your head out of the clouds?" I would have been a stone myself if I hadn't been stirred by what kids like me were trying to do. While stones are weapons, they aren't bombs. I felt I could get behind stones with a clean conscience. The other side didn't use stones to fight back, I promise you. To even the field, our side started to pick up less innocent objects too. That's when I drifted back up into my clouds. Not everyone is made for fighting.

I was the youngest of four boys. My mother always said, "Three for me and one for the cause." I figured, being the youngest, I was okay. Little did I know. Don't get me wrong, I cared about the cause. I wanted liberation for Palestine as much as anyone. I was sick of being caged in, tired of having to shuffle paper to move from A to B, fed up, most of all, of watching my dad struggle to piece together in his mind his decimated village, his father's rock-smashed knees. Most of the time, though, I worried about other stuff. I wanted to figure out this whole girl thing. I was desperate for a girlfriend and thought I was making headway with Sireen. Sireen's hair looked like Medusa's, whose picture I had seen in a book about art my father kept in the glass cabinet with all his special books: the *OED*, *The Times Atlas of the World*, and the one on human anatomy with glossy foldouts. She scared me a little, Sireen. She was wild, I could tell. I was sure we were destined to be together. She lived next door and we saw a lot of each other coming and going. I let my eyes linger. Her eyes would dart away quickly, then come back slowly. I knew she probably liked me too.

There was that. There was also my plan to become a writer and maybe even a professor of literature. I know it sounds oddly specific for someone so young, but it was my dream, what I wanted more than anything. I couldn't really tell anyone. It's not that education wasn't supremely important to my parents. I had heard my father say about a million times that everything could be taken from you but nobody could ever steal what you knew. A degree was a passport to anywhere. Of course, all the education and degrees in the world couldn't get a young Palestinian a job in London or New York City or even Kuwait. That was fine because I didn't want to leave the West Bank anyway. Birzeit University was Harvard to me. Education mattered to my parents – they figured a degree in medicine, engineering, law, architecture. My father loved literature but not as a career for his youngest and brightest. I tried to keep my goals hidden. I wasn't ready to confront my parents. Yet it was impossible to hide my visits to the library or my head in my books at all hours. Even now, if I squint hard enough, organize my concentration on one point just ahead of me, I can almost see myself then, slouched against the wall in the corner of our tiny garden beside the rack my mother used to store green bottles, lost in some novel or scribbling away in my brown notebook, the world blowing up behind my back. My mother would yell at me to step outside the walls of our home. "*Ya Allah*, Nimr, move!" But unless I calculated Sireen would be coming back from or leaving to some place at precisely that moment, I would usually stay put.

Incidentally, I had the coolest name ever. Nimr means tiger in Arabic. I'm sure my parents were highly amused. I can just see them chuckling. While not exactly ferocious, I was moderately dashing with dark eyes that pierced and turned downward like small parentheses. My lips seemed adequate, not too plump like a girl's, not too thin like an old man's. My nose was slightly aquiline but, I thought, in an elegant, ancient Roman sort of way. I was tall, over six-foot, and lanky. I guess maybe I was too thin, not built-up or muscular like my friends. I didn't much mind, though it probably made me less of a tiger than I would have liked. The only real downside to my looks, as far as I could tell, was that I had no hair. That didn't come out quite right. I had hair on my head – thick and dark. I had hair thick and dark in a few other places, too, come to think of it. But I had no hair on my face to speak of, nothing at all on my chest, hardly any on my arms, and only a few threads on my legs. I thought this was painfully unmanly and particularly unfitting a man called, of all things, Nimr.

My friends liked me. They thought my dark humor suited our suspended, crazy life. I amused them even if I annoyed the hell out of them because I didn't list weapons or smoke Marlboros. Mostly I would read to them from my notebook to pass the time. Here's an example of the kind of thing I liked to write:

Ammo *Musa's belly is getting bigger by the second. He swears it has something to do with the water, that the Zionists spike our water with hormones that cause "inflated*

86

belly syndrome." He says they do this because if Palestinians are walking around with inflated bellies, they're not going to be able to fight. When I point out to Ammo Musa that he's one of the few people I know with a belly the size of the Dome of the Rock, he says to wait and see, that it's only a matter of time before everyone starts tottering around like him. I can't get out of my head the image of Ammo Musa and his big-bellied posse, their limbs tied together behind their backs with silk ropes, floating peacefully over Palestine like hot air balloons.

Because my friends were fond of my stories and, for the most part, me, they were usually sympathetic and discreet about the hair thing. But they slipped up enough to alert me to the fact that this hairlessness might be a real problem, chiefly with the girls. It was something I worried about in my fourteenth year and for most of my fifteenth too. That is, until Sireen whispered to me that she liked my glassy face since it didn't scratch hers up when we kissed. But I'm getting ahead of myself.

So how does a fifteen-year-old aspiring Casanova and future Nobel Laureate get himself blown up? To answer I need to go back ten months before the date of my death. I was fourteen and already concerned with the things I would continue to fret over at fifteen – girls, the future, my body hair situation. It was a brisk December morning in 1989. The sky was so blue it was almost black. Rami and I were standing outside my garden wall, Rami smoking, looking as cool as a cowboy, and me standing around with my hands in my jeans pockets. Our high school had been shut down again. We didn't have much to do. I was hoping Sireen's school was shut down too so I could watch her walking home. A couple of kids we knew came up to us and bummed cigarettes off Rami. I had grown up with these guys. Ghassan and Tarik had bullied us all through elementary school. They weren't your everyday, garden-variety playground jerks. These guys had a wicked nasty streak. I had seen them punch kids in the kidneys and cut the tops of their arms with pocket knives. They were angry boys without fathers. Ghassan's dad had been killed and Tarik's dad was missing, either dead or in prison. Their mothers did their best, but they were overwhelmed and tired, and these two were untamable, out in the streets from sun up till sun down. With the *intifada*, they had found their calling. They organized children in the neighborhood. They claimed to have contacts in high places. Maybe they did. They seemed to. I was never one to question the nationalist credentials of anyone, and if Ghassan and Tarik were finally putting their anger to good use, who was I to doubt their intentions? From where I am now, all that patriotic razzle-dazzle falls decidedly flat. But Ghassan and Tarik were scary to me then and I wanted nothing to do with them. That morning, all they did was take a couple of cigarettes from Rami and go on their way without a word. I had a bad feeling.

The next morning, the same scene played over. Rami and I were outside, Ghassan and Tarik sauntered toward us, took cigarettes, then went off without comment or question. My bad feeling congealed in my chest. I could tell they were making some sort of assessment, thinking something through, with Rami and me at the heart of whatever it was. On the third morning, the day before our school was scheduled to reopen, they came along again. This time they stayed. They lit their cigarettes, sucked smoke between their teeth, glanced from me to Rami and back, and asked us if we believed in Palestine. It was nowhere close to what I had expected. I had anticipated blackmail, harassment, some clever form of exploitation, not this demented question about our loyalty to the homeland. I didn't know what to say, so I let Rami do the talking.

"Of course we believe in Palestine!" There was a weird edge to his voice. Rami was a good guy, the kind of guy parents love and parties come to life for. He was terrific to be around because he was always so relaxed. He made everything easy. Plus, he was supremely good-looking. Even more than me. He made the girls swoon. Together we were Robert De Niro and a young Marlon Brando (though taller and without the build). Rami wasn't comfortable around Ghassan and Tarik. Like me, like all of us, he had been roughed up plenty by them. Unlike us, he wasn't afraid of them.

"What kind of people do you think we are? Palestine belongs to us. We would do anything for it." Rami was passionate and adamant.

"Yeah, but would you die for it?" Ghassan's eyes were slits.

"Of course we'd die for it! We risk death walking to school everyday and lying on our asses every night! What are you talking about?" Rami was on a roll.

"Not that kind of death. Would you volunteer to die for Palestine?"

"Like how?" I ventured.

"Like strapping a bomb to your belly and exploding yourself in a café or bus stop or school."

89

I shouldn't have asked. I didn't say anything, but Rami was pissed off now. "Yeah we would. We'd do anything." He shouldn't have said it. I knew Rami; he didn't mean it. But he did say it and he shouldn't have.

"Okay then. You're our kind of Palestinian. We'll let you know what to expect. Good boys."

Tarik was an idiot. What the hell was he thinking? He was no older than us. The whole situation was preposterous. It had to stop immediately.

"Look, we've got to go. My mother's waiting." A supremely lame comeback.

"You go home to your mother now, fierce little tiger. Go on. But we'll be letting you know. We will let . . . you . . . know."

We were in trouble.

I obsessed over what it was exactly that Ghassan and Tarik were going to let us know. Months went by without us hearing a thing, but our encounter still left me frantic. We'd often see the two of them around, and every once in a while they'd give us a sleazy little wink or ask Rami for cigarettes. However, they didn't let us know anything. I spent countless hours rehearsing what it could be that Ghassan and Tarik would want from us. The best case scenario was that we would be made gofers, running between the high-ups and the down-belows. I saw guns passing hands. I saw Turkish coffee with a layer of froth on top served to big men. I saw maps and fake IDs carried furtively from anonymous bunkers to the familiar homes of friends and family. This didn't seem too bad. I could do it, was more than willing to do it, even if it cut into my private time. I would think of it as an adventure, my special contribution to the cause or – why not? – research for my writing. I tried to convince myself that would be the extent of it. But I couldn't get Ghassan's squinty little pig eyes and gravelly voice out of my head. He had said something about a bomb and exploding ourselves in a school or café. It was this, I knew from the acid in my stomach, they would be letting us know.

I created elaborate images of dynamite sticks attached to elastic belts strapped around my waist. I pictured Rami strapping me and then me strapping Rami. I saw us kiss each other on the cheeks and then swat each other sharply on the backs. Then, freak that I am, I watched the front of my pants darken with piss. I saw Rami look away in disgust. I felt myself wanting to stay behind but going anyway. I saw us slip through the soldiers, make our way toward one of the settlements, to an elementary school or a nursery. Rami would always go first. I'd watch mesmerized as Rami blew himself up. His chest ripped away from his back, exposing his broken ribs. His head exploded and made a bubble wrap sound. His insides shot out of his neck in chunks. I saw his body fizzle to nothing. Then I saw the kids. Clumps of their teeth and hair and fingers and toes. Their deflated footballs and burning comic books. Their eyes closed and their small chests collapsing. I noticed pink mist in the air. I heard their screams and smelled their charring skin. Then I'd stop. I could picture my best friend Rami exploding and the stormy little deaths of children. I could plot it all out and, deep down, even enjoy plotting it out. Imagining my own death, however, I could not suffer. I was a coward.

By the end of July, I was still positive we weren't off the hook, but I spent much less time fixated on what Ghassan and

Tarik were planning. Rami appeared to have forgotten all about it as early as a couple of weeks after the incident, and he would make fun of me whenever I brought it up – less and less as the months went by. Though I had relaxed a little and sometimes would go for weeks without thinking about it, I knew, I just knew, it wasn't over yet.

That August I was in heaven. No, not dead yet. Heaven on earth with a *houri* named Sireen. I mentioned before, Sireen and I often played visual pursuit. We'd done so since we were about eleven, the year our worlds split apart. It was the year girls started to play only with other girls and us guys moved away from them completely. I really missed the company of girls, though naturally I hid my feelings from my buddies, who at that point seemed more interested in girlie pictures than real girls. I think I must have always loved Sireen, even when she was little. I would never have said anything to her or to any of my friends, but I do remember informing my mother when I was about six or seven that I planned on marrying Sireen. My mother – I can still see the tiny smile in her eyes – was sweetly supportive. For four long years there was nothing but eye contact between Sireen and me. That summer, however, we were looking for something more.

I was standing with Rami outside my house, as usual. It was hot. We were sweaty. I saw Sireen walking back alone from somewhere. Rami, prince of princes, chose this moment to go inside to use the bathroom. I didn't ask him to, and I don't think he was being considerate. Why would he be? Sireen and I hadn't spoken in ages. As far as anyone knew, there was nothing between us. Sireen, spotting me alone, walked up to me. She did it as if she had been doing it for years. She came in really close. I could smell her. She was sweating too, but her sweat, unlike mine, smelled of jasmine.

"I've been watching you."

"You have?"

"I have. There's a chink in our garden wall. I spy on you. What are you always writing in that notebook?"

"Stuff. About people. And things."

"Do you write about me?"

"I do."

"What do you say?"

"That your hair looks like Medusa's."

"Did you know your lips are the color of pomegranates?"

I remember telling myself to calm my breathing. I felt a grenade in my gut. I felt my shoulders go numb.

"No. I didn't realize."

"Do you think you're going to die young?"

I hesitated. I wasn't sure what she wanted to hear. If I said no, would she think less of me? If yes, that I was some kind of fanatic?

"I'm not sure. I hope not."

"Do you like me?" She was a girl with guts.

"Yes. Very much."

"Good. Should we start seeing each other?"

"Yes."

I found the chink in our garden wall. She had a view of me in my corner. My view of her depended on her mood. Sometimes she would sit coyly on one of the garden chairs reading a book. Other times, usually when her parents were out, she would lie in the grass, her shirt casually scrunched up so I could catch a glimpse of her naked waist, sometimes even the lift of her breasts. Her feet, her thighs, her arms, her neck. I got to know her in pieces. Without planning, we figured out whose turn it was to pose and whose turn to stare through the gap. We had to be careful not to get caught by our parents. It was thrilling. I spent my days and nights buzzing. We would leave notes to each other in the chink. All the writing I had ever done had been for this. If Sireen fell in love with me, it was because of my letters to her. Her letters, less polished, were full of a wildness I had always suspected. That August, we shared a secret in the layers of our skin. Never touching, hardly in each other's presence face-to-face, but always together in writing and in our wall-framed sightings of each other.

In early September, a few days before school was tentatively scheduled to begin – I say tentatively because you never knew when it would be decided that our education was a real threat to Israel's security and had to be postponed for a few days, weeks, months – Sireen slipped me the following note: *Meet me here at midnight*. I thought I might collapse reading Sireen's note, that my knees would give. I pushed my body against the gap, plugging it so she couldn't see me trembling.

Those hours between reading that note and midnight were the best of my life. Everything seemed possible. Ghassan and Tarik were forgotten. Guns and bombs stopped falling. My dead friends and their lost fathers were lazing around in gardens bursting with late-summer bougainvillea. I could hear sea waves because we lived, not in the West Bank, but in the coastal town where my grandfather was born. My brothers and I together made four and not one of us had to be sacrificed for the cause like a lamb. My friends listed their favorite athletes and rock stars. They didn't know what weapons were.

We were hopeful and we were special. We would become doctors and lawyers and engineers and writers and we would change the world and the way people think about the world. We had the luxury to contemplate a universe beyond our borders: starvation and disease, the environment and animal vivisection, other people's wars, but, also, the beauty of stars, the miracle of birds and fish finding their way home. Palestine was a place like any other, where great things could happen.

It wasn't hard for Sireen and me to sneak out of our homes around midnight, to meet at our garden wall. It wasn't hard to walk through our gates, to find a quiet alley in the dark. It wasn't hard to look into her eyes, to touch, finally, the corners of her lips, her neck, her shoulders, her waist, the pieces of her I had memorized. I couldn't hold her in my arms like they do in the movies. Some things are simply too much. Her breath smelled of oranges or apricots, maybe both. She was wearing a white top – was it a short nightgown? – and jeans. We were there for no more than twenty minutes. We hadn't said a word to each other, but right before it was over she whispered, "Tomorrow. Again."

And so it was, in the late weeks of summer or early weeks of autumn, again and again and again. Meeting in the dark alley, kissing parts of Sireen, touching more and more of her at once, whispering questions.

"Do you eat olives for breakfast?"

"Yes. Do you like to swim?"

"Yes. What do you want to be when you grow up?"

"A writer. What do you want to be when you grow up?"

"A mathematician. I think about numbers and shapes. What do you dream?"

"Of you. What do you dream?"

"Of dancing on the beach till dawn in a silver dress."

"Did you know your fingers look transparent in the light?"

"Yes. Did you know you have a face like glass? It makes me want to lick it."

I was at once mortified (my hairless face!) and incredibly aroused (Sireen wanted to lick me!).

As you can imagine, my life that September was a jump off a tall building, a walk under water. Everything fell away or floated around me until midnight. Now I know that the next part had to happen precisely when it did. The devil strolls in when angels get comfortable. I say "devil" and "angels" not because they're here – like the *houris*, they're nowhere to be found – but because they're so familiar, so immensely popular. Looking into your world from where I am, not something I can do with ease – it takes an ocean of concentration and the patience of a mountain – I realize that the minute things seem good will always be the instant the avalanche descends. This is one of the most important insights I've had in this skeletal void. Your parents spend everything they have on a new home; a bulldozer flattens it and crushes your youngest brother. You find the perfect job; your mother gets sick and you must quit to take care of her until the gruesome end. After years of delay, a matching liver is found for your best friend; he dies in a car waiting to get through a checkpoint manned by indifferent soldiers, the hospital fifteen minutes away. These things happen all the time. If you knew how often, maybe you'd stop being able to live. Or maybe you would live for the first time, without devils or angels.

In any case, it came, later rather than sooner, and exactly the way I figured. It was around mid-October and the weather was great – fresh and full of anticipation. Rami and I, at that moment, the sheriffs of youth and glory, were striding home from school. I glimpsed Ghassan and Tarik out of the corner of my eye. Motherfuckers. I wanted to speed up, wanted to run away, was ready to face the humiliation and shame of running away, coward that I was. Anything would have been better than what they were going to let us know. Blowing ourselves up in a school or at a bus stop. Let them jeer and point. I wanted to dance till dawn with Sireen, to feel her lick my face. I wanted to slow down time, to stretch it into the future, to let the past go. But there they were before us, the two bullies of the West Bank, there to blow us up and crush our bones. They asked Rami for cigarettes. I wanted to inhale jasmine and orange. They tried to smile at us, their gray teeth, their slits for eyes. They were telling us they were on our side, the side of our lost homeland. We were going to get it back together. I heard "assignment" and "operation." I heard "outdoor café" and "weekend." I heard "a belt of explosives" and "*houri*s in paradise." I heard words coming out of their mouths I would never have guessed they knew: "maximize civilian casualties" and "venerated martyrs," "tactical gain" and "the greater good." They had let us know, and they would be letting us know more in the next couple of days. "Not a word to anyone. Not even each other." The encounter was over in a flash.

Now I knew. There it was spread out before me, a really bad hand. I wasn't going to do it. I immediately told Rami I wasn't going to. It was a relief to say it after all those months. It was a small liberation, a private expression of manliness to say no. I was a real tiger after all. Rami looked at me like I was insane. "They'll kill you."

"I refuse. I won't and neither will you."

"I'm going to do it, Nimr. I have to. We have to. We said we would. It's the right thing to do. We have to do it for Palestine."

I spent the next two days trying to talk Rami out of it. I didn't believe Ghassan and Tarik would kill us for refusing to kill ourselves. That was absurd. I talked Rami's ear off. I was manic, in a frenzy without limits. I circled around him every second of those two days. Rami was easy, he was relaxed, he was movie-star cool. He threw his head back and cackled. I didn't understand how Rami could be so resigned. None of it made sense to me. Why would they choose us? Didn't these kinds of things take months to train for? How could Rami accept this as easily as he would honey on his bread or sugar in his tea? Maybe Rami hadn't forgotten about Ghassan and Tarik. Maybe he had been readying himself for exactly this.

The third day after Ghassan and Tarik spoke to us, they caught us again walking home from school. "It's set. Tomorrow we deliver the explosives and plans. Day after tomorrow, you execute." And they did. It was that simple. They delivered the belts to us in blue plastic bags their mothers had probably brought home from the fruit market. Right outside my house, casual as cats, they explained how to use them, how to set them off. They detailed exactly how we should get where we needed to be, what time we should depart, what routes to take. That was it. According to Ghassan and Tarik, by this time tomorrow Rami and I and twenty or, if we were lucky, thirty Zionist enemies would be dead. *Allah-hu akbar*.

Sireen and I were supposed to meet in the alley that night. I wondered what she would say about all this. Her responses were as unpredictable as war. I considered telling her but decided not to. That night, everything felt exaggerated – the dark darker, the silence more silent. Sireen was exceedingly beautiful and I was exceptionally horny. I know you're probably wondering how I could have been thinking about sex at a time like that. I remind you that I was, maybe still am, fifteen. Sex and death aren't that different to me. Sex and death make me want to live. And sex is something I think about all the time, even here in the vast beyond. In the heightened atmosphere of that crazy midnight, I wanted more from Sireen than I had asked for in the last month and a half.

"Just a little, Sireen. Just a little." How many boys have said that to how many hesitant girls? I was completely ordinary that night before the most extraordinary day. I wanted exactly what every other boy my age wants. What little Sireen gave me that night is all I will ever have. The same panting and pulsing I now realize every adolescent boy and girl everywhere will feel until we are extinct. There was an eternity between us that night. I thought it was the beginning. I thought there would be more to come, so I pulled up my pants and she smoothed down her skirt, and we laughed together, louder than we should have, our parents, our neighbors so close. It didn't matter. No one was listening that night.

The next day I woke up late, close to noon. I had the house to myself. It was the weekend. My mother would have been at the market, my father at the café playing *tawla* with his friends, and my brothers, the two as yet unmarried and living at home, hanging out in the streets. I took the blue plastic bag and sat in my tiny corner of the garden. This time no books, no notebook. I removed the bomb from the bag as carefully as folding origami. It looked harmless, a contraption I might have put together myself for fun. Sireen was peeking through the gap in the wall. I didn't know that then, but I know it now. Sireen watched as I handled the explosive gently, tenderly, like a lover. It had colored wires going through it. It wasn't very big, and I wondered how much damage it could do. I thought about how to get rid of it. I could bury it somewhere. I could find someone to disarm it. I could explode it in a field. I could return it to Ghassan and Tarik, surely they would understand. I could tell my father, he would know what to do.

My finger caught on a wire. I was careless. It was the last thing Sireen would see, the last thing she would hear. An ambulance came, too late for me, but for Sireen, to try to save her eyes, her ears. A fire truck. The inevitable soldiers making demands and threatening repercussions which, uncharacteristically, never came. I was pleased to learn the operation for that afternoon was cancelled and Rami got to live a few more years. He would die of a brain hemorrhage at eighteen, a rubber bullet to the head.

Things I know now: Life is pomegranate lips. Life should not be Sireen blind and deaf. Life is moist encounters in a back alley at midnight, not boys listing guns, playing with bombs. No promises of heaven and *houris*. Enough. We want to see and hear everything, to dance until the sun rises with a girl in a silver dress. We want to gallop full speed ahead, the sheriffs of youth and glory. Not this darkness, this weight on my chest. Not this ending, not for us.

V

A certain light, hitting the cement platform of the drinking fountains, set hair on fire. If your hair was even the slightest bit brown, your head ended up, at a specific time of the morning, ablaze. It was the kind of light Graham Stevens captured in *Atmosfields*, a 1970s light that shone and blurred, stretched and curled. Light through inflated plastic, to the music of a Bach fugue. We were born into the warmth of that glow, in the year of the dog, though by the mid-1980s it was already being whittled away to the sharp, unforgiving, digital glare of the present.

Catching that light in the morning with our gossamer nets before class set the four of us free. Elsa, Rola, Sara, and me – the Musketeers plus one. We would wait for each other every day on that cement platform. Sara and I, neighbors, arrived together, usually first, then Elsa, then Rola, always last, on the coolest of the bright yellow Salmiya buses, bursting with some kind of news to tell, accompanied by laughter or tears. We would hug, slap hands, hook fingers like we hadn't seen each other in years, every morning a fresh etch to sketch. That early light was a bag of tricks left casually untied. We were oblivious, never grabbing at the flight paraphernalia, never greedy for the tools of escape. Back then, we had our own ways to soar, to cartwheel away – flapjacking, thundersmacking – the four of us with hair on fire. When the weather began to cool, mid-October at the latest, we felt our youth in our throats. In the slats of our flat bellies, our churning hormones howled at us to kiss the boys and make them cry, as many as we could, quickly, quickly, our glittering locks urging us on. Out of the corner of my eye: Jonas at the gate like a starfish, a seagull, a Baltic wave pounding through gilded light. In he came, and the world opened as if forever.

~

Bear

This will be a love story. It is set in Kuwait, but Sweden hovers in the background. Unlikely collision between desert girl and snow boy. In a small leather pouch carried every day for a year: a secret disclosed too late. This is a story of endings.

Does she write this for him? One year, five years, two decades plus pass. Time's relentless march. Short brown hair and a red sweatshirt around her shoulders, sleeves flipped back like a scarf. In the places that count, Mina remains the same. He once wrote, fifteen years later: *You're still fourteen years old, pretty as a flower, with great expectations about life, love, and the future. As I'm writing this, I suddenly remember the kiss on the deck.* Time marches and stops. Some events freeze solid and remain hidden in pockets to be taken out and fingered after five, fifteen. Even twenty.

Mina and Jonas sitting in a tree k-i-s-s-i-n-g. Last comes love. Too late.

The kiss on the deck of a stationary ship. The kiss in an elevator. The kiss on a bus before goodbye.

A dream, lately, about another kiss photographed. A lost snapshot glimpsed between the pages of a book in a dream and the rest of the dream an attempt to locate this phantom photo between the pages of a phantom book. A desperate attempt to recover that photograph, to stop time, to capture a patch of impossible infinity.

She imagined him in Swedish snow then, and imagines him that way now. Jonas with the white kerchief tied around his neck and his striped shirt blue and white. She had wanted to untie that white around his neck. He would walk in late. Five minutes before the bell. Three minutes. One. She would be there earlier, watching the gate. Always with the lanky haloed boy. Sunshine Peder racing in and Jonas, always slower, hanging back with an indulgent smile. It was Peder who would sweep her off her eager feet, kiss her on the cheeks, her red sleeves flapping. Every morning bright kisses. But not from Jonas of the white kerchief. Did Peder know then, in October, December, January? Were Peder's kisses Jonas's? Peder could not resist lifting her up by the armpits. A lift, then a kiss. One too many kisses. Sunshine Peder faded to black. Jonas from the land of snow stepped forward.

What he had said to her was this: "In ten years, you will still be here. You will be married. You will have children. You will always be in this place." Offhand, with smug certainty. She would prove him wrong. She would escape the trap. *Je refuse!* She had refused to stay put. To marry. To have children. But she had, more than ten years later, closer to fifteen, come back. Kicking and screaming. She had returned to take over someone else's responsibilities. Bird feeding, heart mending, memory gathering. How could he understand? It would

106

require too much to untangle. To understand takes time and time has passed. Five, fifteen, twenty. He would smile again, slow and indulgent. In ten years, you will still be here. You will always be here. But there are no children and always is a long time. Never too late. Too late for Jonas and Mina sitting in a tree.

She couldn't understand his skin, his floppy brown hair, his gray-blue eyes, light brown eyes, hazel green. His skin more vibrant and darker than a snow Swede's should have been; his hair not blond enough; his downward-curving eyes, color now forgotten, more sad. But maybe her own sadness was there, not his. He was happy and floppy. A singing Swede. Drinking and taking in the dizzying Arabian sun. It didn't belong to him. It wasn't his trap. A one-year reprieve from snow. But there was brooding in those downward eyes, she was sure. A young man's passion and arrogance and irony and, in droplets, his insecurity, piercing the way only a young man's could. It disappears soon enough, replaced with a sticky, eye-rolling confidence. It goes away, the young man's feminine beauty.

She thinks they officially met after she already loved him, waiting for him to walk through the gates. Maybe it was the contrast to Peder's ebullience. Maybe they were in a class together. Maybe it was because he carried little things in his pockets, mysteries he would take out once in a while, look over, then put away. He kept a little black notebook. Once they were friends he let her peek in. It took many months for him to show her. Inside it he wrote in tiny script, baby ants across a shrunken page. The marginal illuminations were tiny too. Persian miniatures in watercolor. Smaller than a postage

107

stamp, the size of painted rice. An artist, it seemed, so more broody, less floppy. She loved him before the notebook, probably. But that notebook clinched it.

She had forgotten about the bank, about the island escape. He loved her, in other words, in other worlds. He reminded her later, after five, ten, fifteen. They had agreed to rob a bank together, to escape to an island. Sea and sand and time to love. To seek solace in a cliché as only young lovers can. They were never lovers. It was far too early for that; he knew better than she. Both too early and already too late. Clichés become a lifeline. The island with its sand, sun, and breeze, its hammock and unfolding future. "Maybe we could rob a bank together. Maybe you will leave this place after all. Maybe I will take you to an island in the sun." Secrets in a small leather pouch and on islands that still, to this day, intrigue. The mystery of the leather pouch she knew all along.

It was in his pocket with the notebook, the other objects. Out it would come. The leather pouch fingered gently. "What's in the pouch, Jonas?" The downward curve, the vibrant skin. "What's in the pouch?" The Cheshire Cat smile looking up or down. It happened maybe once a week. Sometimes he would be sitting, other times standing. But the fingering, gentle, tender, that was the same. And the same question, "What's in the pouch, Jonas?" The Cheshire Cat smile till she had had just about enough and would throw water at him from the fountain or run away for him to run after her, into the playground like the kids they no longer were but still, sometimes, wanted to be, into the darkened locker room that one time.

The bite on the arm was an act of love. The bruise left behind an insignia of faith. Of that she was oblivious then.

Then, it was a chase during lunch. Rushing into the boys' locker room where they were not supposed to go. The space dark like a hotel room. They were still panting, still laughing and tumbling, but they knew they had arrived at a moment. The stillness of a vortex point. Still panting but not laughing, looking up into downward eyes and looking down into *what exactly?* Did she have her arms around his neck without the white kerchief that day? Did he put his arms around her waist? Did he lift her and kiss her? She must have been wearing short sleeves. How exactly did his head bend down, then down some more, lower than she would have thought, past lips and chin and neck and shoulder? Did he kiss her first? A kiss on a bare arm in a white uniform shirt? Dark and silent, with kids laughing outside, running around the playground, throwing water from the fountain, giving chase to boys. Boys catch girls. Three, two, one. You're it. Did he lift her chin up with his artist's fingers? Their first silence. No panting, just breathing or holding breath. Four, five. The bell about to ring. Then the coil sprang. His head, lower than she would have thought, his mouth closing in, his teeth biting down hard on the flesh of her arm. She screamed and splintered the hush. This time he ran. She stayed and looked down at the strange sign of his love. She rubbed his saliva into her skin and, for the next week, wore the badge of his teeth marks with pride. Phantom kiss.

February, March, and she kissed others in sand and ice, in hidden stairwells. She knew he had a girlfriend, maybe two or three. She still would wait, heart pounding, for him to walk through the gates, but she would leave before he could approach. Maybe there were other moments. Maybe they sat together during algebra. Maybe they walked to class together. She remembers him tripping on steps once on the way to class and herself laughing at this unexpected interruption. That fall was a gift to her – his vulnerability, his shyness afterwards, his body splayed like a pinned insect. A long dancer's body with artist's fingers. She laughed but he didn't, which made her remember he was a kid after all. Eighteen is still a kid. Maybe it was then, February, March, that they stopped running, that they became friends.

It seemed invisible for months, March, April. It might have had something to do with the warming weather. The sun and sand and smell of freedom and fun and not being bogged down with the weight of love bites or loaded clichés. Lifting does not belong to blue spring days. She in her world. New Wave and boys and a love affair with the beach. Sun-baked pleasure with the girls, laughing together in the sand and sea. Waves of the blue-green Gulf. Unfurling together at the Sea Club. An island escape. She would not conform. A bikini is a weapon. *Je refuse!* In the Arab world, a bikini is a slap in the face, a stare down, a face-off, a go to hell in a hand basket. She learned then to wear her body without shame. *Look at me. You are invisible.* Laughing with the girls in waves and kissing the boys they decided were pretty enough to kiss in the breeze. Count them: one, two, three.

She in her world.

He in his.

A French girlfriend with bouncing blond hair. *Oui.* A coquette in the French style. At the Sea Club sometimes, a flip, a wink. *Voila!* How to compete with that? Smitten with the pretty French girl with the glass giggle. Jonas fell for the icicle blonde, delicate as tulle, *la* French *belle*. At least for a while and not too hard. Drinking, as young Swedes do, in the sun. He in his world peeking at her in hers.

The pouch disappeared. She (almost) forgot about it.

It was the year of the furtive whispers by men who were old enough to know better. The year she smelled of freshly cut grass in a country where landscaping is a luxury. She stretched out, all promise and exuberance. No illnesses, no deaths, no prohibitions, yet. No attempt to save time. No reason to follow the phantoms of desire, of photographs lost. Everything poised to begin just then, the vortex point. A stillness beneath pulsing flesh. Mina was, in this final year of late childhood, already the adult she would become minus the damage of the onward march. There was expectancy and quivering. Music drifting out of windows left open on purpose. White curtains flapping like red sleeves in the dry breeze. The word girl's flesh and blood. It was the year of airports imagined for later. Taking flight. In ten years, you will still be here. You will be married. You will have children. You will always be in this place. *Je refuse!* In the breeze carried in by the long white tails of open windows, she refused. In the words she writes, even now, she refuses to let the phantom go.

Maybe this is the story she has been rehearsing her whole life. Why this moment? Why this pouch? This stationary deck? This elevator? Why this goodbye before flight? Why this snow boy's kerchief-tied neck? This bite like a badge? This dizzying sky, Arabian blue, before the fires, before the end for us, before death and damage and no going back. Frozen in him, Mina becoming, not what she would become (for now, but not forever, please, never forever; she still

111

refuses!). Frozen in the snow, still unfurling, arms outstretched, expectant, land still open and hot. In snow there is no war. No prisoners made to stand like crosses, unspeakably smeared. No inexplicable cancer. No oil under the desert more beautiful without it. No plastic byproducts dimming the blue-green. No holy moly abracadabras one, two, three, you're dead if you don't bow down four, five times a day. Jonas from the land of snow with a pouch that contains everything from before. There are days when the pouch opens. A tear in the constellation letting old light in, blue-greens and downward-curving brown-grays. A talisman in the pouch hinting at, promising, reaching toward something, anything that hasn't come before, that doesn't feel somehow, yet again, familiar. In his slow walk from gate to building, in her anticipation of what might or might never follow a bite is everything we ever hope for. A constellation of sparks, a tapestry woven over the years, strand by glittering strand, a life. And then, suddenly, a tear in the constellation letting old light in. This could break her heart. Or maybe it is just what she needs, just what she has been waiting for. Maybe it is what we need to stop dimming seas, naked crosses, multiplying cancers, holy moly abracadabras, the oil in the desert breaking the world apart. Just what we have all been waiting for.

He gave her the leather pouch, before the kiss on the bus, before the envelope unopened, before the final flight on the last day. The pouch, after the kiss on the deck, after the kiss in the elevator, the first real goodbye. Silence between them on the deck, words unsaid. The French *belle* gone. Mina and Jonas sitting in a tree. Finally. April, May, June. Jonas of the snow, floppy still, insecure but piercing. A young man with young skin and a dancer's body, artist's hands. The boy lost for words but piercing still. Electric fingers locked and thumbs caressing. Looking out at the blue-green, seeing only black, at a dance on the deck of a stationary ship. Waves licked the sides of a ship aching to move, to escape the trap of land, anchors aweigh to sail on the merry sea, now black with night, to the land of snow and ice, elsewhere. Murmurs and whispers. They stammered to each other. Straining to hear them. Half-sentences, half-words strung together like popcorn, paper chains, a feather necklace. Pretty. Stars. Far away. Island escape. Fragile. Tonight. Trembling. Snow. If only. Language failed. Silence like before the phantom kiss. This time Jonas kissed Mina, opened her throat for shushed sound to emerge, eyes closed but flickering to see them kissing for the first time, slowly, slowly, all the time in the world to kiss her lips. Never again such excruciating beauty, electric fingers, open throat. Never again like that, black sea ahead and stationary ship. Before goodbye, that kiss. To save between the phantom pages of a phantom book in a dream. Forever is a long time.

It was everything they ever imagined it to be, and after, fingers still entwined, they walked underwater to the elevator. The elevator, like the end of the world, the end of joy, the end of everything before the final storm. The elevator she imagined would crush them. It would preserve them like fossils, suspended in that first perfection, perfect only because it came first. An elevator on a stationary ship soon to be burned in the war of oil and cancer. An unruly elevator where elevators had no business being. On a doomed ship, their chariot. In the elevator, another kiss. Time stopped. Would that be it? She would remember. The best year of her life. Would this be the final k-i-s-s? Jonas and Mina. Not forever. Last comes love. Words failed.

Jonas said goodnight to Mina. It felt like the first honesty. Looking down into a car, downward-curving eyes, sad, a prelude to the final goodbye. For Mina, he broke, for a second, unexpectedly. That was the night of their first kiss and second to last. It was the end of the best year ever. No promises were necessary when the future was still unfolding. They didn't understand possessiveness yet. No promises were sought when all it took was a blue sky and laughter in the waves with girls. There was no premonition of the pain that would descend, also in waves. *Après toi, le deluge.* Even in that, excruciating beauty. Tears that flood the body for the first time since, lucky girl, never before a loss, an illness, a death. *Not lucky for long.* The first realization that love is possible, that some versions of life might not be, that an island escape may vanish. Forever.

The car drove away in the dark and Mina was not yet a doll in pieces, not yet pencil shavings on the floor. Chatting with the girls in the car about the dance and fairy dresses and the prettiness of the first time. Muted chatter for Mina who sank into throat opening, lips pressing, eyes fluttering, over and over again. Stop. Rewind. Stop. Rewind. All she thought it could be and more, more, more. It was the future in her hands. The promises – unsaid, unnecessary – little colored candies in twists of crinkly paper, hers to open. All hopeful and trusting and prepared to jump and no looking back and happy. Mina bouncing like two transparent rubber balls, pink and green, higher and higher. The sound of promises

114

unwrapping, about to be made, hope not yet let down. The world still a peachy sunrise to a girl with red sleeves flapping, with joy like spring rain on rare desert grass. On that drive back home from the dance, Mina was pink and green, not yet in pieces.

Then, one week later, the final goodbye, the secret of the pouch revealed. Jonas walked in through the gate alone and for the very last time. He moved quickly. He looked directly at her, serious, furrowed. Fifty meters, thirty, twenty, ten. The distance between them closed. She saw something in his left hand. Was he left-handed? Memory's collapse, but a tear in the constellation. Mina stood at the edge of the pavement watching Jonas walk toward her. Nobody else existed. Nobody breathed. He stopped, this time looking up. He held open her hand and placed in it a small leather pouch and a square blue airmail envelope. *What happened next?* Her fingers closed around the pouch, smaller even than she remembered. The envelope slid into her pocket, unopened. He took her by the hand, the same hand holding the pouch. They cradled the pouch between their fingers like love, fragile, on the brink of breaking. They walked together to the gate in silence, hand in hand. The heat, the noise of buses ready to leave, ice cream vendors on all sides shouting, "Zoom, Zoom, Zoom. Lolly, Lolly, Lolly." The final time he would hear these words he has heard every day for the last year. Would he forget? Has he forgotten now? Someone got on a bus. It was him. Hands still clasped, he kissed her on the mouth. In a Muslim country, he kissed her deeply in front of everyone, on a bus about to leave. The world was invisible. "Zoom, Zoom, Zoom. Lolly, Lolly, Lolly." Kids were screeching for summer vacation, arms were dangling out of buses, ice cream was dripping. In the heat of June there were no words, there were no tears. A downward-curved goodbye.

Mina walked back, tracing their steps alone. Past the pavement, past the boys' locker room, past the water fountain, up the steps into the abandoned school. Hallways bereft of kids were suddenly gray. She walked into the bathroom, into a stall, locked the door, and leaned back against it. She breathed in, the pouch cupped gently in her right hand, the unopened letter in her uniform pocket. The tenderly fingered leather pouch, his arm, his neck, his smile, his dancer's body, his artist's hands. The school was empty. She could hear the buses leaving. She would be left completely alone. She lingered, slow, indulgent. To open the pouch was goodbye. The end of childhood, the end of the first time, the end of laughter in waves, the end of the secret. Opening the pouch was Mina unfurled. Jonas took with him the promises unsaid, wrapped in crinkly colored paper, the first kiss, the second to last, the last.

She opened the pouch, took out its contents. A wooden bear with a small smile. Jonas had made this. He had carved it. He had painted it. What's in the pouch, Jonas? A bear. A bear I made for you. A Paddington. A Pooh. Because I'm still just a kid. Because I don't want to let go of the smiling bear. I'm letting it go.

Maybe he thought she would be able to cradle it for a few more years before she too would have to let it go. He was wrong. That was the last year for Mina. She carefully put the bear back in the pouch and pulled the unopened envelope out of her pocket. She slid a ruler under the flap. A small

116

rectangular card with a bear painted on it. In the belly of the bear, tiny crawling ant script. *My Dearest Mina*. My dearest. She stopped reading. The most dear to him. Mina. She continued. The letter unfolded love. Faith. He had not told her because he knew if he had it would have been impossible to say goodbye. He had decided not to act and so, all year, floated in a kind of purgatory. *But maybe*, he wrote, *in another time, another place. Maybe on an island together.* Resorting to the cliché. How many loves missed? How many people in the world to love, but never? How could he have withheld a year of new love, maybe the best, maybe just ordinary? He loved her. She, the most dear to him that whole year. The word girl's heart raced. Alone in an abandoned school, Mina with a bear in each hand.

For the next five years, once or twice a year, Mina would get a postcard from Jonas. His cards were always brief, energetic, elsewhere. The bear secrets were never mentioned. Jonas of Arabia was gone, back to the land of snow and light. No wars of oil and cancer for him. No dimmed blue-greens, no plastic byproducts, no holy moly abracadabras. Jonas fades to black.

It isn't Jonas that matters. After ten, fifteen, twenty. Jonas disappears, but the secret stays. A tear in the constellation. We remember, we remember, the place where we were born. Gone forever. Dimmed. But sometimes. The most that can be hoped for in this land of oil and cancer: a tear and a bear letting old light in.

VI

In 1984, smoking was allowed on airplanes. It's baffling to us now. Just imagine the reek of it. But back in 1984, there we all were, clumped together at the tail end of a British Airways Boeing 747-200, smoking like tomorrow was never going to happen to us. Look at us, golden, drinking champagne, vodka, red wine, whiskey, beer, whatever, out of clinking bottles and mini cans, screaming with laughter (when things could be that funny). Smoking and drinking, limbs knotted, making out at the back of an airplane. The stewards and stewardesses – they weren't yet flight attendants – handing us endless bottles and cans, knowing we were parched. So what if we were fourteen, fifteen, no older than seventeen? So what? They weren't much older than us and they sympathized. We were staggering out of a desert. We deserved it and they knew it. Once in a while, they took drags off our cigarettes, sips from our bottles. They were with us. They were on our side. Don't ask how we all managed to sit together, kids from three different international schools in Kuwait. Kids we didn't necessarily know personally, but had seen often at the skating rink or at parties. Now we had our arms around each other, were sharing each other's saliva; and after the summer, we would pretend none of this had ever happened, like we couldn't quite place that face. I don't know where our parents were. In the middle of the plane? At the front of the plane? I don't know how we managed to congregate at the tail end together like that, without having to answer to anyone. Flying doesn't work that way anymore. No more. Flight attendants are serious. Cockpits are bolted shut. Smoking is strictly prohibited, even in lavatories. But flying out on a Boeing 747-200 in 1984, to better places no doubt, the future was an egg, our egg, on the horizon.

I'm not sure he was with us on that particular flight. I put him there now because he was beautiful. He was so tall and he belonged to our school; we could be proud of that. ASK was for the lucky ones, for the kids with bones that glowed, pulsed with promise. Nader's arms and legs would not have been knotted with mine on that flight. I hardly knew him, though I remember him completely. He had the ease of an older brother – protective, lasting. I want Nader on that plane with me, with the champagne, with the rosy light along the horizon, early, early in some-body's morning. I want to see him leaving Kuwait for the summer, following the promise of his beloved stamp collection. I want to see Nader again, young and arrogant, tossing back his chestnut hair, laughter in his teeth.

After that summer, in the relief of autumn, Nader would be found by his parents. Nader, hanging naked in his family's garage. Imagine all that beauty, long, loose limbs, the hair of a fucking angel, swinging gently in a cotton breeze. Think of the parents, their precious boy. His hands tied together with wire behind his back, this was no suicide. Who would kill Nader? It's the easiest thing in the world to rumor drugs. Easy to think it, easy to mutter it under your breath. We did, though we didn't want to believe it, his naked body burned in us forever. To crush that kind of splendor so early in the game for drugs or money is obscene. On that flight, it still wasn't possible. Nader is there, smiling sweetly at the blonde stewardesses taken with his olive charm.

~

Elephant

Stamp

Adam's father, they were told, vanished without a trace. It was like he had melted into the horizon, leaving behind nothing but the residue of his good deeds as mayor of the village. *Jido* Thomas had packed no bags, had left no letter, apparently, had given no warning to anyone that he was planning to go anywhere. There was no way of knowing whether he had suffered a stroke or some rare form of amnesia in the night. His behavior the day before had not been unusual. Beiruti police were alerted but, accustomed as they were to mysterious disappearances and kidnappings those middle years of the war, they weren't keen to pursue the case of a missing grandfather, a man in his late seventies. They did, however, ask to be informed if a ransom letter appeared. For filing purposes.

In the ensuing chaos of planning a trip to the village to see for himself what might be done, Adam didn't think to ask his son about *Jido*'s final letter to him, though he had been the one who had handed it to Nader three days earlier. Adam and his wife Nadra, used to the playful and innocent missives *Jido* Thomas had written to a younger Nader, never considered that the exchanges between grandfather and teenaged grandson, exchanges they no longer read eagerly over their son's shoulder, may have developed into something deeper. They certainly never imagined that Nader's last letter from his grandfather might hold the key to the old man's disappearance. Years later, when it no longer mattered, they would find out it did.

Before all this, Nadra and Adam had always considered themselves lucky. They belonged to a village buoyed by a glut of good fortune, so their luck felt natural to them. The pair walked through life with kismet on their side, but their chests remained resistant to the spread of pride they had been cautioned could take down the hero of any land. None of their people had thought to warn them about the invisible perils of luck itself, however. None had bothered to mention that sometimes, maybe once every couple of generations, luck becomes a curse.

Nadra was eighteen when she and Adam married, but she had known him long before then. She knew him because their fathers and grandfathers shared arak and apricots under the village pines, listened together to cones cracking in the high afternoon sun. She knew him because their mothers rolled grape leaves side by side on the narrow shores of a nearby stream, molding graceful green tubes from long rice and unhurried dreams. Nadra knew Adam because his sister linked arms with her as they skipped to the songs their grandmothers sang to them in the light whisper of evening, songs about the forest at dawn, about learning the language of birds.

Lebanon then still offered itself believably as the empress of the Middle East. To drive up into the mountains in the morning to ski and then to swim in the Mediterranean all afternoon was the lush promise it never failed to keep. Money poured in from across oil-sopped deserts. Banks and casinos swelled and lifted spirits and not even the sky could limit the certain goodness of the future. Lebanon was the place of blue and yellow light, of honey on warm almond cakes, of girls and boys with a ready spring in their step. Nadra and Adam were there, and their world pledged miracles.

Adam had ideas, but in his village his family had clout. The string of priests and politicos threading their line meant that he and his three brothers, like their father, the mayor, or their uncle, the town priest, had one destiny or the other already in store for them. The rusty ache of religion and politics was as familiar to them as it was to every Lebanese, though some years it burned less than others. The year Adam turned fifteen, life in the village took the shape of a snow crystal and everyone was beaming with azure hope. Adam, as inflated with expectation as everyone around him, announced to the villagers one balmy August evening that he was going to fly. With flashing eyes and a heart as full as it would ever be, Adam explained to the puzzled group, gathered together for their monthly communal dinner, that he was going to train to be a pilot for Middle East Airways.

The villagers fell silent and still, frozen at odd angles. Adam's father walked toward him, his sharp blue eyes pinning his youngest son like a butterfly under glass. Adam did not flinch.

"You, like every one of your brothers, like your father, like your father's father, like your father's father's father before him, will be a priest or you will enter politics."

"I," Adam replied, "am a pilot."

The villagers, still motionless, sucked into their lungs the faintly wet night air. The mayor of the village gazed into the untroubled gray eyes of his youngest son, the happiest eyes he had ever seen in his life, impossible eyes that seemed oblivious of history's ruin. He had done something right with this boy.

"And," Adam calmly continued, "once I'm done studying, I will come back to the village to marry Nadra Issa. I will take her with me to Beirut as my wife and we will have three children together, a boy and two girls."

Up to this point, Nadra Issa, George Issa's only daughter, had been standing unnoticed off to one side of the orange grove. Suddenly, though certainly not for the first time in her young life, Nadra found herself the object of the villagers' attention. She was just as astonished as they were. To be singled out by Adam, fair-haired charmer of the neighborhood, was special and Nadra knew it. He wasn't the best-looking boy in the village; even his brothers were taller and more dazzling. But watching him in the field where all the boys spent slow afternoons kicking around some coveted ball, Nadra had noticed Adam's wide capacity for fun, his mischievous self-assurance. Adam was a notorious flirt. He could make every girl who crossed his path feel like she held magic in the palms of her outstretched hands for ten minutes at least, sometimes, if he was in especially good form, fifteen. Nadra struck him as different if only because she tended to stare hard at parts of his body and to ignore most of what came out of his mouth. Through Nadra's sea green gaze Adam traced a route out of the village, a life strung up above clouds, beyond the heft of time. Nadra, twirling an orange blossom fast in her fingers, laughed out loud when Adam made his confident claim, but when he looked over at her, he caught her approval in the easy swing of her hair. Adam knew Nadra was his.

The mayor recognized Adam wasn't asking his permission and, contrary to what everyone in the village figured, his son's audacity did him proud. He took Adam's face in his hands, kissed him hard three times on the cheeks, and ordered him to name his first child after its mother. This Adam would gladly do.

Adam's plan unfolded exactly as he wanted it to, and in 1965 he and Nadra were married in the village church by his uncle. Nadra had always possessed the luminous beauty of the mountains, even as a baby. The women of the village – and, furtively, their husbands too – enjoyed watching her grow into her skin, milky as a September moon. They tittered together about the effortless sway of her adolescent hips, the early fullness of her breasts, the playful arch in her lower back. Forms of beauty that would make most people in the world gasp for breath were hardly blinked at by the villagers, accustomed as they were to its reflection in the landscape. They attributed this abundance of beauty to the special luck that distinguished their village, and though they never neglected to sing their gratitude to the Blessed Virgin, it still took something extraordinary to capture their attention. Nadra was extraordinary, her uncommon poise conveying to them all on a daily basis the meaning of her well-chosen name,

Nadra, rare. Growing up, Adam had always been aware of Nadra's beauty, but it was the humor in her raised brows that drew him in, the knowing self-possession of her olive stare that convinced him she was special. On their wedding day, Nadra, orange blossoms in her hair and secretly barefoot beneath her long white dress, was, to Adam and to all the villagers, everything fine the universe made possible.

The only way to convey 1965 Beirut is to picture a putty-washed technicolor postcard of a sequined sea in a tangerine light. It felt like discovering a private cache of someone's love letters or learning it was possible to live forever. Beirut was the overwhelming desire to lick a lover's wrists, the eternal yearning for a first kiss. On its sun-soaked streets: curly-haired cherubs running through, not a care in the world; vendors on corners selling aniseed ices and *kaa'k*; the scent of thyme carried on a breeze, an intimation of marinated meals to come. That year, in the splendor of their fabled Paris of Arabia, Nadra and Adam's marriage was golden, setting a mighty precedent. It was the year of Nadra in a vanilla bikini that offset her caramel tan. It was the year of waltzing in dance halls, smiles as wide as the noon sky, with friends unimaginable the year before, friends as sophisticated as the French they all spoke with such remarkable ease. 1965 was the year Nadra and Adam would force themselves to forget, refusing to allow its extravagance and flash to break the rest of their lives.

The following year brought rumblings of a future few were ready to face. Nadra and Adam, living comfortably enough, had not yet deposited a single lire into the savings account

Adam's boss had advised him to open the day he was hired. The collapse of Intra Bank, therefore, meant nothing immediately personal to them.

"What does it mean to run on a bank, Adam? I've never heard of such a thing? What is it that we are expected to do?"

"Nothing, my angel. Not a thing. We'll go to the kino tonight, and afterwards we'll dance and drink champagne. Don't bend your head over anything, *habibti*. This is Beirut. It bounces."

Nadra believed Adam. She always did. He kept to himself the fact that, as Intra Bank was a major shareholder in MEA, its fall could very well threaten his livelihood. Shot through with Beiruti confidence, Adam was convinced a mere bank failure could do nothing to halt his rise, his airline's rise, his city's rise to the peaks of the highest mountains. How could it possibly? How could anything?

Adam lived like nothing out of the ordinary was happening all through 1967. The only events that mattered to him that year were getting Nadra pregnant, welcoming their first child into the world, and naming him Nader, after his mother, just as he had promised Thomas. The wrath churning around them was ignored.

It was impossible for Adam to ignore 1968, however, since Israel's decimation of the Lebanese civilian air fleet directly affected his everyday life. Allowing himself to feel the revenge of time snapping at his country's heels, fearing its inevitable crunch, Adam made the excruciating decision to leave Lebanon. He packed up his wife and his son and together they returned to the village for a week of goodbyes. His bewildered father was heartbroken and refused to see him, refused

131

to acknowledge what he saw as a violent and unnecessary severing of ties. Adam's mother worried her son had lost his bearings, and Nadra's parents wailed for their girl as though she had a terminal disease. Adam, accustomed as he was to flight, to an airplane's routine telescoping of time and space, could not understand this immoderate grief. Even with his deep sorrow over Beirut – a sorrow that would haunt him increasingly over the years despite every attempt to blot it out – he was excited to begin again, excited with a feeling of expanse only the young own. The future belonged to them. They would go to the boomtown of Kuwait where everything still seemed possible, if twenty degrees hotter.

Climbing up the steps of an MEA Comet temporarily chartered from Kuwait Airways, Adam swore on the head of his son Nader – an oath he would live to regret – that he was washing his hands of politics and religion forever. If he had paused to listen just beyond the strident reverberations of his own voice, he would have heard his wife's small, dizzy whimper. Cosmopolitan as she had lately become, Nadra remained a girl of the village, never proud enough to tempt destiny's cords to tighten around their lives. To hear her precious son's head used as potential collateral, especially on such a poor promise, filled her with a murky-toned, all-consuming dread. Unlike her husband, who seemed more and more relieved the further away from Lebanon they flew, Nadra soared through the air toward Kuwait with tiny black birds of trepidation circling her pretty shoulders.

Kuwait was on the up and up. It was a place eager to learn about pleasure from Beirut. After centuries of desert dwelling and pearl diving, the recent gush of oil promised great bounty,

unprecedented advancement, a life of plenty for anyone interested. Adam was interested, and he put in the hours at Kuwait
Airways, worked harder than anyone to turn it into a compet-
itive airline. Plus there were striking black-haired girls in mini
skirts. There were dance halls and drinks. There was an international school for Nader and an equestrian club with pris-
tine beaches where weekends could be spent lounging with
friends. Fun was in the air and Nadra quickly forgot her early
apprehension about leaving home. Once the war began in
Lebanon, not so many years later, she and Adam, a safe
distance from the fray, couldn't help but feel luck, their old
friend, on their side.

The only dark patch on their otherwise incandescent existence was that Adam couldn't seem to get Nadra pregnant
again. A boy and two girls was how Adam had pictured it in
those warm days of adolescence. Some mornings, over breakfast, he wondered whether naming their son Nader, rare, had
initiated an altogether different trajectory for his family than
the one he had so carefully plotted. But he refused to allow
the words "fate" or "destiny" or "God's will" to punctuate his
thoughts. He chose, instead, to focus on "luck." They were
lucky they had one at all. There were countless couples who
didn't even have that. Brushing all doubts aside, Adam would
slurp up his sweet Turkish coffee with immense satisfaction,
bang his small cup loudly on the table to hear Nadra call to
him from Nader's room that if he broke her favorite set he
would be buying her ten more to compensate. He would don
his pilot's hat with a flourish and, from habit, thank the
Blessed Virgin for all the luck that was so clearly his.

*   *   *

133

It all started with a letter addressed specifically to Nader from his grandfather in 1972, on the occasion of his fifth birthday. The letter itself was brief, even a little stilted. It was, after all, the first time Thomas had ever written to a grandchild, the only grandchild he would ever have to write to, the others never leaving their village. Over the years, his letters developed a style Nader would come to adore. Through the energetic language and elaborate stories relayed about who in the village had done what to whom and for what unfathomable, ancient reason, he discovered his *Jido*'s wicked humor, his formidable authority. Behind his grandfather's large, confident scrawl, Nader sensed an intelligent evenhandedness he hoped he would one day inherit. But all that would come many, many letters later, after an avalanche of letters, sometimes one a week. Thomas's first letter, a line on white paper transparent as a single ply of cheap Syrian tissue, didn't convey much at all to Nader. *Happy Birthday my grandchild,* it said, or something as innocuous. What caught Nader's fancy was not the paper or the words, which he couldn't read. What caught his attention were the stamps on the envelope commemorating the Munich Olympics: black silhouettes of athletes performing Herculean feats suspended in colored ovals. Nader couldn't take his eyes off the images – those vibrant rings, all that power quivering beneath taut muscles, the ink lines marking the distance crossed from Lebanon, a place he did not remember, and home. He was more fascinated by those stamps than by any of the expensive toys bought for him by his parents and his parents' friends. To Nader, collecting the stamps off his grandfather's letters felt like capturing stars. His big black stamp album promised a world of adventure and, together with his father's tales of Bombay, Rio, Athens, and Rome, conveyed to the boy something of life's great allure.

That first letter arrived in the middle of September, a few days before Nader's birthday, a few days after the Munich disaster. Adam considered whether his father was trying to tell him something with those stamps. Had he bought them months earlier, using them now only because they happened to be in his rickety desk drawer? Or was he hinting at the state of things, at approaching catastrophes swirling like smoke in the air across the Middle East and up into Europe, as far away as Munich? In those six pleasing stamps, far more than he needed to stick on, was Thomas signaling his approval of Adam's decision to move his family to the relative safety of Kuwait?

It wasn't that Thomas ever completely stopped speaking to his son. It was true he had refused to see him the week before his departure, a snub registered by the villagers as a definitive sign of an irrecoverable love. But they were wrong, and even that lonely week, Thomas had silently slipped a sealed letter into the hands of his wife. His wife, his partner in all things, needed no special instructions. She folded the light blue Aerogram into a neat square and placed it in the inside pocket of her son's jacket, the pocket where she knew he kept photos of her, his father, his wife, and his child, photos that ensured he would not be without those he loved if ever the planes he flew failed and went down. Adam opened the letter as soon as he found it. All it contained was a phone number and a fat scribble: *Once a month.*

The first few calls were stiff, not least because Thomas was unaccustomed to speaking into a device. The odd time lag between his voice at home and the voice of his gray-eyed child so far away took some getting used to. Thomas, now officially *Jido* Thomas, at first used questions about Nader to deflect attention away from the rift between Adam and himself. Incapable of cutting off contact completely, *Jido* was equally unable to let things go. As patriarch of both his family and the entire village, total forgiveness would have been interpreted as a sign of weakness, and Thomas was still lordly enough to care about appearances. This would change.

Adam learned to read the stamps on *Jido*'s letters to Nader as coded missives. He grew convinced the Munich Olympics stamps indeed signaled *Jido*'s acceptance, if not approval, of his son's move to Kuwait. A moss green stamp of little boys in red shirts playing football gently probed the possibility of more grandchildren. Adam would never have the heart to explain to his father that Nader was destined to be an only child, fulfilling the promise (Adam still refused to see it as a curse) of his name. With Adam's brazen vow on that unforgettable afternoon still ringing in *Jido*'s ears – a boy and two girls – *Jido* knew his son would have done all he could to make it happen. In *Jido* Thomas's stamp of the footballers, Adam didn't read disappointment or reproach but, rather, all the things he would have less of: a father's hand through his child's hair; the sweet sweat smell of that child after play; a small voice in the middle of the night asking to be let into his and Nadra's bed. But he also read in that stamp, and in so many others, *Jido*'s sympathy and, more than anything, his love for Adam and his little family.

Nader, unlike his father, didn't bother to decipher secrets from his grandfather in the stamps. He didn't need to look for

136

hidden meanings since his correspondence with *Jido* was unobstructed, frank, often sharply humorous. Nader's interest in the stamps had to do with something else entirely unconnected to *Jido*. When Nader saw the stamp *Jido* had stuck on one of his letters from 1975 – an image of the jackal and lion from the *Kalila wa Dimna* tales – what unfolded before him was that devilishly wide and unanticipated world of books and their clever enchantments. This was not about the usual catalog of children's books he was more than familiar with from the library at the American School of Kuwait. This was not *The Hardy Boys*, not *The Famous Five*, not even *The Wizard of Oz*, though that last one might have come closest to the new realization brought on by the *Kalila wa Dimna* stamp. Nader, fascinated by the meticulous illustration of the proud, almost jolly looking lion and the emaciated jackal with the flapping jaws, immediately asked Adam about it.

"They're a collection of short tales about the lives of animals, some of them noble, some of them trouble. They tell us things about how we should live in the world."

"Where are they from? They sound Arabic. Who are Kalila and Dimna? Which one is the lion?"

"Kalila and Dimna are both jackals. They show up in most of the stories, that's why the collection is named after them. It's hard to say where the stories are from. They're from a bunch of different places: India, Persia, Iraq, Spain. It's interesting because the stories changed as they traveled from place to place. That's how things are, Nader. Everything collects traces. You're no different, you know. You're a magnet attracting life filings as you grow."

"I think I'd like to read *Kalila wa Dimna*."

Adam happily bought Nader a copy of the stories translated into English, the language his son was most comfortable in. This didn't bother Adam the way it did Nadra and some of their friends, who all feared their children's loss of Arabic was going to exile them from Lebanon even more. Adam wasn't convinced there were degrees of exile. Plus, he believed languages were for everyone. It didn't matter to him that English rather than Arabic or even French was the one Nader had chosen for himself. Nader had already made it his own in the way he wrote to his *Jido*, mixing it into the Arabic his grandfather preferred, making both languages vibrate and keeping *Jido* on his toes. As it turned out, Nader would become fluent in all three languages anyway, moving through each like a Kashmiri shawl through a rose gold ring. *Kalila wa Dimna*, even in English, gave Nader a sense of the wide open world and the role the imagination could play in shaping it. It made him realize that things were more connected than they were apart, but also that not everyone could see or wanted to see the links. Nader would come to believe that sometimes it was prudent to keep the links invisible, that some connections weren't meant to be shared.

To Adam, on the other hand, the *Kalila wa Dimna* stamp *Jido* had chosen for that letter sent just at the start of the civil war, a stamp that had commemorated the *Journée de l'Enfance* a few years earlier, had nothing whatsoever to do with literature and its strange worlds. It certainly had nothing to do with children or their designated day. Adam understood immediately that with this stamp his father was making a political statement, warning of upcoming betrayals and chopped up lives, of jackals that would trick lions and of lions that would make unlikely demands on hares. Adam could sense – despite the dreams that still came to him in technicolor, despite the endless promise of his glorious boy – their old world rapidly plugging up behind them like a drain. For the first time in his life, Adam began to register promises in pieces.

But even with Beirut on the verge of a calamitous war, Nadra and Adam had each other. And they had what mattered to them both even more than each other, as they admitted without jealously or resentment: they had Nader. Nader shimmered with an appetite for everything around him, and it was this quality, more than his incredible good looks, that drew even strangers to him. Nader's atmosphere was, like all atmospheres, mostly illusion. His was the ephemeral atmosphere of Kuwait in the 1980s, still seemingly untainted by clawing, meddling neighbors and the dank fumes of righteousness. That a Christian Lebanese boy could encapsulate this chimerical time in such a volcano of a place said it all. But even then trouble lurked in the shape of black-eyed hawks and bearded beasts, types Nader would have read about years before in his illustrated copy of *Kalila wa Dimna*. He would be long dead before these forces would shroud the country, but his weary parents would be there to witness Kuwait's atmosphere, like their son's, vaporize to nothing.

In August 1984, a month before Nader's seventeenth birthday, a month before his death, he was on a plane heading to New York via London. He was going to visit Columbia College, his school of choice for after graduation the following year, a graduation that would never come. Adam was piloting the flight. About midway through, he emerged from the cockpit to stretch out his legs, to survey the people whose fragile lives were, for a brief time, in his hands. As he walked through the plane, he caught a glimpse of Nader in a seat close to the back. He would never in his whole life forget the scene before him. His son was at the center of a group of young people. Everyone's attention was on him. He seemed to be describing something, his long, fine hands making odd shapes in the air, of cars or planes or, perhaps, lions and jackals. There was a young girl with exquisite features sitting on his armrest, and every once in a while, his son would ruffle her bobbed hair affectionately, the sister he never had. Periodically the group burst into laughter together, a single organism unified in the promise of youth. In one month's time, at the end of September, *Jido* Thomas would have been missing for two years. Seeing his radiant son on that plane, Adam knew in his bones, in a way he hadn't allowed himself to know until that moment, he would never see his father again. His glamorous son on that flight – surrounded by all those young people, a glass of something in his hand, making them all roar (when things could be that funny), heading toward something in front of him (how was Adam to know it was death?) – made it possible for Adam to let his own father go.

The phone call relaying *Jido* Thomas's disappearance stunned Adam. For weeks after he moved around like an anaesthetized ghost. Nadra feared for her husband's well-being, but she feared for Nader's more. She remembered with a crash Adam's long-forgotten oath on their son's head to be done

140

with politics and religion. She was certain one or the other was the cause behind *Jido*'s vanishing. She worried Adam would be sucked into a mess he knew nothing about and that demonic forces she still believed in, still a village girl at heart, would descend to extract the price. Suddenly, here was Lebanon at their doorstep, and they were not equipped with the necessary dexterity to maneuver through its deadly tit for tats. Slowly, slowly, Nadra and Adam began to feel their luck changing.

Nader, on the other hand, had been expecting it. Not precisely his *Jido*'s disappearance, but something. The arrival of *Jido*'s final letter preceded his vanishing by three days. The date marked in blue ink over the magnificent stamp revealed that it had been posted a week before that. Nader debated whether or not to show it to his parents. A lesson he had learned early on slipped into his head: some connections were private. He could not betray his *Jido*, the grandfather he rarely saw but whom he loved and who, he knew, loved him with the grandness and gentle wisdom of elephants.

The letter made *Jido*'s disappearance easier for Nader to accept than it was for his parents. He knew, even after two years, their world was not the same, and he regretted his invisible role in their prolonged grief. That morning of the call, Nader decided to hide the letter under the center of his mattress where he knew his mother's nimble fingers couldn't reach it accidentally while changing the sheets. He didn't believe his mother, or his father for that matter, would ever purposely snoop. Nader was certain *Jido*'s last letter wouldn't fall into their hands, an eventuality *Jido* had warned vehemently against. In his final, desperate moment, Thomas chose to confess to Nader, a fifteen-year-old boy, and not to anyone else because he was aware of the double helix in his grandson, a spiral blend of lightness and gravity that ensured he would protect the last actions of a broken old man.

Fourteen years after her son's death, Nadra found *Jido*'s last letter to Nader hidden under his mattress. It had been placed right in the middle where her fingers, still tucking in clean sheets every week for the last fourteen years as they had for all the years of his life, never reached. If they had, they would no doubt have found, in the luck-filled early years, a few *Playboy* magazines, notes scribbled on scraps of paper once spiral bound from girls desperately in love with her chestnut-haired beauty, a joint or two, and, every once in a while, a stamp that promised Nader something about the future he wanted to remember. Nader had thought of his mother's fingers the morning he selected where to hide *Jido*'s final words to him; and Nadra, panting a little with the exertion of pulling her son's old mattress off the bed frame all alone, ignoring her husband's earlier plea to wait till he got home so he could help, knew it. Nadra collapsed into her boy's dusty, dump-destined mattress, now taking up half the floor. The thought of Nader contemplating her fingers was a thing that could rip apart the tight stitching holding her together. She simply could not allow herself to unravel on this day before their return back to Lebanon, forty years after making Kuwait their home. She would not do it to Adam. She focused instead on the letter in her wilted hands.

Adam had never shared with Nadra his belief that *Jido* Thomas spoke to him through the stamps on his letters to Nader, but looking at the stamp on *Jido*'s last letter Nadra came to the same conclusion. *Jido* had been trying to tell them something. This stamp, fragile and sad, stood for goodbye. It was smaller and less flashy than most contemporary Lebanese stamps. It looked like it could have been from the colonial period. Not Lebanon's, but India's or maybe Kenya's. The stamp was monochromatic, an unearthly teal. It looked a little like those stamps of Queen Elizabeth that seemed to come in endless colors – though Nadra wasn't sure quite how she knew that. Where the Queen's face should have been, an elephant's appeared. It was in profile, nothing but one large ear, a lowered trunk, and one steady eye. It was the eye that got Nadra. It looked exactly like *Jido*'s. It was as though *Jido* had somehow managed to etch his own eye into this most incongruous, unlikeliest of stamps. The elephant looked like it was about to speak. *Jido* seemed plaintive, diminished. And in the mournful, glossy eye of her father-in-law, Nadra saw the reflection of her son.

19 September 1982

My dearest Nader,

It is impossible you have already heard what has happened.

Every year begins with hope in this village. We give thanks to the Blessed Virgin despite ruination, despite injustice. But after this, hope is finished. I cannot begin again after this.

The blackest stain. You will hear of it. Sabra and Shatila. They were trapped like vermin, hundreds of them, maybe thousands, surrounded and slaughtered. Even if it had been only one. The blackest stain.

Blessed Virgin.

Two girls got out. Twins. I heard about it from the judge, the one with the white beard and blue eyes, remember him? You once said he looked like God. They found them in a cellar two kilometers from the camps. They refuse to speak. I can't stop thinking about these two girls, eight, maybe nine years old. They could have been your sisters. They are your sisters, Nader. They are my granddaughters. These two girls quaking in a damp cellar with no food or water, centipedes in their tangled hair.

How could we?

I've included a list of names. There is nothing you can do with this list. I don't want your father to see it. It is absolutely imperative, Nader, that your parents do not see this letter or the list. No matter what happens, this is between you and me. When your father chose to leave, he made the right decision. I couldn't see it then, but I see it now. I will not allow all this to drag him back into it. He is free. You are his freedom.

But this list is something I want you to have. I want you never to forget who's who and what's what. Maybe you will never return to Lebanon. Never return. But if you do, I want you to know.

I'm going to look for those girls. I'm a dead man with this list, but I have to see the girls. If there's anything left for Lebanon, it's in them.

This will be my final letter. I love you.

Goodbye.

Thomas

VII

Sara once gave me a tiny gold ring with a speck of emerald on it. It may have been for my birthday. It may have been for friendship. It fit, just barely, around my ring finger. Sara had hair like a Brillo pad, at least that's what Jake and Andrew said, every single day, twice a day, for about two years. We weren't sure what a Brillo pad was, what exactly it looked like, but we knew it wasn't good, that it implied something harsh and kinked, something to scour black pans with, a cruel exaggeration of Sara's hair. They called her Brillo pad and me Mona Lisa, which sounds a lot better but wasn't. Yellow-eyed Jake and red, flaky Andrew – cherry orange hair, pale pink, freckled skin – you know the type – horrible, diseased-looking, but saved, swelled, and made cocky by his Americanness. Not much we could say to counter that.

When Sara and I were younger, Jake and Andrew ignored us. But by the time we were around eleven or twelve, we were worth poking and prying. For them we were an untapped version of fun. We weren't mice, Sara and I. We would poke and pry back – mocking yellow eyes and splotchy red skin. But with a single "Oh yeah, Brillo pad?" or a solitary "Watcha lookin' at, Mona Lisa?" we were screwed in our places. Sara was self-conscious about her thorny hair, and I was unsettled by being likened to Mona Lisa who, I had read, might actually be a man and who, in

145

any case, had a sneaky smile. For a year or two we put up with their unpleasantness.

Girls change suddenly. At fourteen or fifteen they can become minxes without notice. After one long summer, Sara marched onto the bus wearing the kind of lush beauty – red-lipped, olive-skinned – that makes cars honk and boys (and girls) gasp. I boarded after Sara – all high cheekbones and newly angled arms – and Jake and Andrew, slack-jawed, fell over themselves trying to blot out years of teasing and to replace it as quickly as possible with a new, awkward fawning. Sara and I, blotting out what we could of Jake and Andrew – so much smaller than we remembered them – talked, with striking animation, about the weather.

At the end of the year that we morphed into minxes, I exchanged Sara's ring for a small leather pouch. The ring was the only thing I had on me that I cared about, the only thing I could give to Jonas that last day. Sara was not happy and considered my gesture thoughtless, frivolous. What Sara never really understood was that giving away my emerald ring said more about my love for her – black-haired beauty – than my love for him.

~

Her

Straw

Hat

Julie may have been the saddest-looking woman ever to board the hydrofoil, Flying Cat III, from Athens to Sifnos. Yannis couldn't figure out why Flying Cat? Flying Dolphin, Flying Fish, Flying Octopus all made sense. Flying Cat made no sense. It was the sort of detail Julie would quietly notice and record in the big black ledger Yannis knew had to be tightly wedged inside her head. She would put it in the section called "Inexplicably Annoying Details I've Come Across and Have Refrained from Commenting On." Yannis was convinced that would be one section among many in Julie's black book. An especially thick section would be titled "Even More Inexplicably Annoying Details I've Come Across and Simply Could Not Stop Myself from Commenting On." Once upon a time, Julie's complaints had rushed through their lives like a wind stream. Yannis wished it was that way still. Anything was better than this sadness, shaming and acute. Julie's sour odes used to make him chortle, had signaled to him she was engaged with the world. Not happy, but engaged, anchored in, clamped to land and to him. Now, Julie was adrift. She was floating. Not yet drowning, but she was clearly not flying. No flying cat, his Julie.

Her sadness as she boarded the hydrofoil was so leaden, he feared the ship might sink too deep. He worried everyone in the cabin would feel the weight of his wife's misery, that it would smother their youthful excitement about the summer, about all that sex waiting for them on the islands. Surely they could sense the saddest woman in the world had just boarded. Surely they would presume, their sunflower heads twisting toward Julie, that it was all her husband's fault. The man accompanying the saddest woman in the world – lanky and tall, teal blue eyes and sandy hair – must be responsible some- how. Yannis walked around with the guilt over other people's silent accusations thudding hard against his back exactly the way the waves now thudded against the side of this boat, this incomprehensible flying feline.

Yannis saw to it that the children were settled in. He put Zoé in the aisle seat in front of him, fastened her seat belt and showed her how to tighten it around her five-year-old body. Jules sat in front of his mother, in the seat by the window. From his backpack he took out a book – one of the thick Harry Potters – and his rubber clown's head, which he began to rub rhythmically against his forehead. He sucked his thumb hard; he had been waiting to do it for hours. That morning, Yannis had informed Jules he would be allowed to suck his thumb once they got on the hydrofoil but not a minute before. So Jules had been counting the minutes from their apartment to Charles de Gaulle, the plane ride to Athens, the taxi ride to the port at Piraeus, to this moment, this heavenly release on the wondrously named Flying Cat III. Sucking his thumb and riding on the back of a flying cat all the way to Sifnos, better than a broom, better even than a hippogriff or thestral. Yannis knew Jules, at eight, was too old to be sucking his thumb, but since he was the son of the saddest woman in the world, Yannis figured the kid deserved a break, deserved to take whatever joy from wherever he could for as long as the world would allow. He wondered whether Jules's sucking bothered Julie, whether it was noted in her "Have Refrained from Commenting On" section. She would sometimes watch Jules as he sucked, rubbing that grinning clown's head hard against his own. Her eyes would narrow as she stared at her son. At his sucking? At the impossibly large head snapped off the strange rubber doll she had bought for him before he was born? Did Jules trouble her? Yannis had no idea.

Jules was such a good boy, maybe the best boy ever. He said the kinds of things that made his father remember curiosity. Jules asked Yannis why humans didn't have wings to fly like bees or why they couldn't breathe underwater. Jules thought it would be splendid if stars were connected by a pulley system that children could hold on to and then swing from constellation to constellation. Jules was attentive and generous, rarely short with his little sister, never once jealous of the attention she had drawn away from him, at least in the beginning, before it was taken away from them both. He was patient and quiet, could spend hours alone reading or examining things under the microscope Yannis had bought him for his birthday, demanding nothing from anyone. Julie's silence and her sadness were accepted by Jules without judgment. Yannis sometimes caught his son's eyes, worried like beads, caressing his mother, loving her with his gaze but asking for nothing, knowing, maybe instinctively, she had nothing in her to give. His son was an angel, and when he smiled, too rarely, his dimples twinkled like stars in a twilight sky.

Zoé had a small pink backpack precisely the size of her back. She was a tidy little girl, pond brown eyes, sandy blonde hair bobbed and fringed. More a doll than a child. Zipped up inside her backpack she had puzzles and books and bright plastic capsules she collected from the center of chocolate eggs. She had a scrap of blanket she dragged everywhere with her, to school, to parks, to the market, to bed, on flying cats. She sucked her thumb, like her brother, and she rubbed her tatty blanket scrap against her nose. Zoé's voice carried. She could be quiet for hours and then, suddenly, loudly, she would ask a question or demand attention, unaware of the way her voice rippled her family's stagnant silence. But now, on the hydrofoil, she was as quiet as her mother. She held her scrap against her nose, her thumb in her mouth, her four other fingers out like a small fan. She would sleep for the three hours it would take to get to Sifnos.

Julie pulled a book out of her purse with a gesture that mirrored her son's. She was glad Yannis was handling the children, smiling at them, doing what a good parent should do, everything she could not do herself. She pulled her knees close to her chest and ignored everything around her. She tried as hard as she could to ignore Yannis sitting beside her, taking apricots out of a plastic bag, the excruciating way he bit into the fruit and allowed the juice to drip over his lower lip onto his chin, not wiping until a second before it would have been too late. It was maddening, but not enough to say anything about, not enough to break her cocoon of silence. She didn't have the energy for that, for speech, for chitchat, for tenderness. It was simply too much. She wanted only the comforting parameters of the dumb novel in her hands. No more than that. She hadn't spoken a word since the morning. Yannis had done everything. He had packed for the kids, for himself, for her. He had made the children laugh as he dressed them. He had checked all the faucets, switched off all the lights, pulled out all the plugs from the sockets. He had called a taxi and taken out their suitcases. He had locked the front door and pressed the button for the elevator. He had checked them in at the airport. He had bought the tickets for this ridiculously named hydrofoil to Sifnos, Flying Cat III. Not I, not II, but III.

Julie could not bring herself to speak. Not a single word. Not even when she had seen him pack that tattered straw hat of hers, the floppy one with the thin red ribbon around its brim.

Julie had been wearing the same hat on the blazing afternoon she boldly – bolder than ever before – placed a Mythos at the tips of Yannis's long fingers. That was twelve years ago. She was twenty-seven years old then and had decided to go to a place she was certain no other Kuwaiti would be and, if she was especially lucky, no other Arab either. None of the people she had asked had ever heard of Sifnos. They had heard of Santorini, Crete, Rhodes, Mykonos. But not Sifnos, not her secret Sifnos. She wanted out of the trap of Kuwait, the burden of its rights and wrongs. That place – the broken Middle East – often felt foreign to her, an uncomfortable elsewhere. She wanted to have done with everything she felt to be irrevocably beyond her: the desert, the black poison oozing beneath, the white scorching sky, the ominous eyes of judgment and, most of all, her parents. At least for a while. She was sick of the mystery behind her mother's sadness, her father's indifference. She was fed up with the guilt her parents made her feel with every loaded sigh, every slow blink of their drained lids.

She was named Ghalia, expensive, because she had come after many miscarriages, stillbirths, early baby deaths. The price paid for her existence may have been her mother Salwa's emotional balance, her sense of justice and goodness in the world. By the time Ghalia was conscious of them, her parents were utterly detached. To be in the presence of her mother felt like being at the foot of a great Icelandic glacier. She couldn't ask anything of her; her enormous silence took over every room of their tight house but one. Only Ghalia's room, with its door firmly shut and locked, her radio, a calming box of noise, always on, provided some reprieve. Ghalia's father, short and exhausted, offered nothing much to counter his wife's neglect of their daughter. Rashid was ordinary. He worked at a bank, like many Kuwaitis. Not a swank bank job but a dull one with no chance of advancement. Rashid didn't care. He wasn't ambitious. He wasn't much interested in anything. There was no hidden key to his indifference, no lurking childhood damage or psychological potholes. Rashid drifted and rolled, wanting nothing more sensational than for his days to squeeze through.

In his whole life, Rashid had done only three incongruous things, the first when he was seventeen. After graduating from secondary school, he had decided to move to Paris to learn French. He had stayed for two years and returned fluent in a language that had nothing to do with him. He had studied business administration at university, got his brainless bank job, married Salwa without ever having met her, and tried everything he could to get at least one of her many pregnancies to stick, convinced the babies died, one by one, because he didn't love his wife. He had never visited France again and never told anyone at the bank he could speak French.

Rashid's second incongruous act had been to enroll Ghalia in the French School of Kuwait. He had vowed to speak to her only in French, a language Salwa could not understand. This hadn't done much to lure Salwa back to the land of the living. At the French School, Ghalia, one of the few Kuwaitis there, was christened Julia and nicknamed Julie. Ghalia insisted on being called Julie all the time. Since her mother rarely spoke to her and her parents had little to do with their extended families – Ghalia's vague army of aunts and uncles, her two sets of grandparents – she could easily forget she was once Ghalia, the expensive one. She slipped into Julie, into a life of milky coffee in the mornings and small, pastel-colored *petits fours glacés* in the afternoons. A charmed French life in her head: Astérix and Tintin, *cahiers* and *stylos*, lavender billowing in the summer rain, homemade yoghurt in small, glass jars. Julie, with long brown hair, eyes as dark as destiny, and a winsome overbite. Julie, not tall, not thin, but hourglass voluptuous as a teenager and after. Julie in Kuwait with her head in French clouds.

At twenty-seven, Julie had saved enough money working at a bank – not the same bank as her father, a better bank, a better position with better prospects – to take three months off. She had been traveling to Paris for a couple of weeks a year, every year, since she had started working at twenty-one. She didn't want to spend her three months there. She wanted something as incongruous as her father's stay in Paris had been for him all those years ago. She imagined Greece, slow, indigo or cobalt blue waves that looked snowcapped marching knowingly from island to island. It would be warm, not just the temperature (nowhere, after all, was warmer than Kuwait) but the landscape itself. Cliffs with goats proudly perched, winding roads, arid mountains scattered with olive trees, pulsing with bougainvillea. An orange lava heat that made skin bloom beautiful, too good to be true. She chose Greece because it was everything she was not. She was cold, more like her mother than she cared to admit; it was hot. She was quiet, though not yet silent; it was loud, its wind a symphony orchestra. She was contemplative, almost reptilian; it was urgent, like a motorbike or a black wasp. She wanted to spend three months in a place nothing like her, nothing like her mother or her father, nothing like her country or her people. She wanted to be at the edge of an unfamiliar cliff, to jump into waters that knew nothing about her, to be anonymous, transparent, cast away. Sifnos was that place.

Yannis stretched to touch his wife's arm, to offer her an apricot. She could muster only the smallest shrug in return, the slightest shake of the head. He let her read. She was grateful for that, eternally grateful for Yannis's discretion. He never mentioned depression, Prozac, psychiatrists, psychologists. He could have easily. He was a doctor, an internist. He knew many doctors in Paris. They were a close-knit group and he was well-liked, his Greekness an asset, his Frenchness, for a foreigner, impressive.

Yannis knew to back off. He always knew with Julie when it was best to back off and when it was best to inch forward. Rushing never worked. Except that first time with the beer daringly deposited at the tips of his fingers, glimmering butterfly wings she had said. He had just turned thirty and had decided it was time to return to the island for a visit. Yannis had fled Sifnos at seventeen, had gone to Paris to become a doctor. Nobody on the island had been able to understand it. A doctor they could understand, the island always needed an extra doctor. But Paris? Why so far away? Why not Athens? For his parents it was as if he had taken a Turkish dagger and twisted it into their eyes. He had felt the guilt they wanted him to feel, had trained him to feel, in waves, but he had been too young to allow it to change the direction he wanted his life to take. His relatives, his family's friends and neighbors – the whole island, really – all decided Yannis was marked from the beginning, a northerner at heart, blond, blue-eyed, almost Swedish. A loner, whispered the friendly ones. An anti-social, wayward sort, squawked the less kind. Yannis, like many island boys (and some girls from Kuwait) wanted out of the smallness, the inquisitive gossip, the incestuous involvement. He wanted to do things that everyone around him had not already done a million times before for thousands of years. So off he went to Paris, a doctor in the end, not coming back for over a decade.

That slow summer of his return, he had been waiting for something, waiting in one taverna after another along Platys

Gialos. When Julie arrived with her beer, her floppy straw hat with the red ribbon around it, that impossible story of hers – a girl from Kuwait with a mother as silent as stones and a French-speaking father – in Sifnos of all places, he hadn't been surprised. It was like a tight conclusion to a story. The Kuwaiti girl (she would hate that) with the floppy straw hat. Everything about her already in that hat shading her brooding eyes, her dark hair. Later she would tell him that what had drawn her to him was his blondness, his teal blue eyes – she had never known eyes could be teal colored before – his tall lankiness, his quiet calm. He was so Scandinavian. She liked that he didn't need props – a novel, a cigarette, backgammon – to sit and stare out at the sea. These details had allowed her to be forward with him, to get herself entangled enough to decide this was it. They both had decided quickly, island boy, red-ribbon girl, that this was it.

The third incongruous thing Julie's father had done – after learning French and sending his daughter to a French school – was to give her easy permission to marry Yannis. She had brought him home with her after the three months on Sifnos, something a typical Kuwaiti girl would never, ever do, might be killed for doing. Her parents, still isolated, still as distant as peace, had not been perturbed in the least, were even dimly satisfied their daughter was finally getting married. People never tired of telling them that twenty-seven was almost a spinster. Yannis had converted to Islam on paper, not for her parents, who didn't care, but for the law of the land. Julie had quit her job, packed her life, said a formal, clipped goodbye to her parents, her few friends, and moved to Paris, plunging, it seemed, into French clouds and lavender fields, away from glacial sadness forever.

Yannis vowed to be patient this summer. Her mother had jumped out of a window just four weeks ago. Her mother was dead and her father didn't seem overly distraught. Only three days after Salwa's death, Rashid's daily routine had gone back to normal. Bank, home, bed, interspersed with a few words to Julie in French and silent pats like afterthoughts on his grandchildren's heads. It had been hellish with the children in that house in Kuwait for the two worm-like weeks of their stay. For three days immediately following Salwa's suicide – the three days he imagined Julie wanted nothing more than to be left alone with the space left by her mother, now even more silent than stones – masses of people poured into the house. For three unending days, all the obnoxiousness in the universe oozed through the front door. People told Julie how sorry, truly sorry, they were for her loss, how she had to put herself in Allah's hands, to be strong for her father and her children. Yannis would be patient this summer, but he knew that Salwa's leap out of a window – a suicide that was a sin in Islam, condemning her to a hell neither she, nor her husband, nor her daughter, nor he, for that matter, believed in – was not the cause of Julie's silence, her setting adrift, a pumice floating alone on dark water.

Julie's silence had started a few years after Zoé was born. No. If he was truthful, it had started exactly after Zoé was born. Julie began taking longer to respond to questions. He would catch her glowering at nothing in particular, a valley between her brows, and he would have to repeat her name

159

two, three times before she would acknowledge his voice, his presence. She stopped smiling, that quick flash that could light the world, never frequent to begin with, soon completely absent. Sex came in droplets, water forced from bricks. She didn't want it, he could tell, but even the effort to refuse him required too much of her. He couldn't stand feeling like she was doing him some terrific favor, allowing him to stretch into slick pockets. To have to ask for sex is a diminishment, a pathetic little death. For Yannis, the last five years were obliterating. There were no kisses, no embraces. He still reached to touch her arm, her thigh, her belly. He couldn't stop himself, pretending he was trying to get her attention, but just wanting desperately to touch any part of her, to grasp the memory of straw and red ribbon. He recognized Julie becoming Salwa. She had told him all about her absent, blotted-out mother, boxed in a cubicle nobody could access. He could see it happening to Julie. He was a doctor, of course he could see it. But she was so grateful when he said nothing, when he left her alone.

Yannis was forty-two. They had been coming to Sifnos every summer since that first summer they met. He was tired now, exhausted. He wanted her to snap out of it, to help him with the children, to fuck him again. He wanted to desire her. Not just her. He wanted to desire.

There it was, the island rising before them. He prepared his camera. He collected these shots, these yearly advents. They would stay at a hotel in Platys Gialos, not with his parents. He couldn't tolerate their noise, their prying, their meaning well, their invasion of Julie and the children. He wanted to stretch out – a flying cat, yes, why not? – on the hotel lounge

160

chairs. He wanted to feel his skin burn, to feel the breeze cool it off. He wanted to stare at the half-naked bodies of young girls from behind dark sunglasses like some oily, desperate man. Sometimes he wanted to be as silent as Julie. Other times he wanted to create the grandest ruckus the island had ever seen or heard. He wasn't certain yet which way the summer would go.

Julie would turn forty this year. She felt fifty, maybe sixty. When she was fifty Zoé would only be fifteen, a minx with an hour-glass figure like her own. How would Julie manage it? She was already so tired. She had no humor left in her. She knew she was at an impasse. She knew they were too – her husband and her children. They could have been together, four starfish together in an underwater paradise. It seemed impossible now. From the moment of her daughter's birth, Julie had felt pursued by a gaping mouth with sharpened teeth catching at her clothes. For the first two years she had managed to wrap any flapping material tightly around her body, mostly flying clear of the sticky teeth. But before long Julie found herself sinking deeper and deeper into that gaping hole. For a while she had managed to rejoin the other three, perfection under glass, for months at a time. But too soon there was glass rising between them and her – at first clear, then more opaque, more and more crackled, finally a sandblasted mess. She wasn't sure anymore. She was evil. She was lost. She was floating away on clouds without borders, no place to speak of, nobody left, nobody from the very beginning for Ghalia, for Julia, for Julie. A Kuwaiti girl in a French school. How could it ever have worked? What had he been thinking?

*   *   *

161

At the hotel, Yannis got them all ready to go down to the pool, a pool at the edge of a cliff. He sat on a wooden lounge chair scrutinizing the pretty girls spread out before him like cards. He turned briefly toward Julie. His wife's eyes seemed closed, the air around her dotted with ladybugs. What would having that blonde one there change? He stared at her without shame. Would a push between unfamiliar, elastic thighs make him feel younger, if only for a hard second? The blonde looked up and noticed him staring. Yannis did not look away. She lowered her sunglasses slightly and surveyed him from the top of his head down to his toes. She pushed her sunglasses back up, flipped onto her stomach, and untied her white bikini top.

Julie's eyes were half-closed. She didn't mind. It didn't bother her that he looked, that he desired something about them, maybe the curve of their calves or their sharp clavicles. "I love the way your hat casts small shadows around your clavicles," he had declared to her when she spoke to him for the first time, when she had offered him a beer, a gesture he hadn't realized then was audacious for her. She had laughed out loud, her teeth exposed, amused by his specificity. She cringed now to think of that hat packed away at the bottom of her suitcase.

The blonde girl stood. She sauntered toward the changing room. She glanced back at Yannis. He considered following her. Julie, he predicted, would turn away like air. He stood too, stretched his arms above his head. He wasn't sure what to do or what he wanted. Julie's straw hat.

He had never been as happy as when she had come to him that first time, except for when the children were born, his

162

Jules and then the miracle of Zoé, after months of Julie laying flat in bed, her mother's bitter history of misbirths flapping shadows around her shoulders, those precious clavicles, all the while. He was not exceptional. A good doctor, but not exceptional. A good husband, lover, but not exceptional. A good father, he tried to be exceptional, but he wasn't convinced he was or that they, his two, would remember him that way. Julie was adrift, cast away on a different island, a different planet, maybe on a star burning inside out. They would remember her vacancy always, and they would not remember him as their savior.

He glanced toward the changing room. She was still in there, perhaps waiting for him. He edged toward it like a thief. He could hear his children speaking to each other.

"Regarde! Les poissons, là!"

"Où? Quels poissons?"

"Là, là, regarde bien!"

What fish? How could there be fish in the swimming pool? But Jules insisted, directing his sister's head toward the skimmer, the dark, rectangular shelf in every pool that shoots an electric bullet of fear into the hearts of children everywhere. At first Zoé didn't want to look into the hole, but her brother took her by the orange arm puffs and propelled her to it. She peeked inside.

"C'est vrai, c'est vrai! Il y a des poissons! Trois petits poissons! Regardez!"

Jules left Zoé bobbing in her orange floaters, her turquoise swimsuit one size too big so it would last two summers, head tilted to one side, gulping fish with her eyes. He ran to tell his parents about the improbable fish. Jules, confident, open, thumb unsucked after a few hours in the Sifnos sun, ran along the wet edge of the pool. Yannis turned to Julie. She fixed her obsidian eyes on him and, for the first time since he could remember, she smiled.

She watched Jules run toward his father's wide open arms. What if he tripped and cracked his skull? What if Zoé panicked alone in the deep end and choked her small lungs? What if Yannis had a heart attack, a stroke, a car accident in a tunnel? What if, on a sharp blue day like today, the three of them took a helicopter to another island and it fell out of the sky? What if Yannis decided, at last, to take the children and walk into the sunshine? She shut her eyes, inhaled desperately the sharp Meltemi wind.

Julie remembers walking up to Yannis in her straw hat, its thin red ribbon fluttering in a lulling breeze. She wants him, his fingers on her thighs, her scooped, half-moon belly, her arms lifted above her head, elbows back like a taught bow, like a bird. She wants him to watch her as she struggles to come up for air, for his hands to hold down her hips, to anchor her, to keep her from drifting. She wants him to speak to her in lilting, foreign French, sometimes unexpectedly harsh, with a word that could as easily be Arabic as Greek. She wants his northern light, misleadingly northern. She assumes he is from Stockholm, Copenhagen, Oslo. But even after she finds out where he is from, she wants the incongruity – her father's girl – of his northern fairness and his languid, southern solidity. She wants. She desires. And when Jules is born, she wants him too. His ten fingers and toes, tinged blue at first, then rose, his teal blue eyes, his round head crowned with blond wisps, his dimples twinkling. With Zoé it is different. On a bed for months, blood dripping slow, then infuriatingly fast, then slow, thinking only of her mother, how they have no language to connect them, the cord cut by her father, by French, too early, far too early. But for months on that bed, checking the rate of drips every fifteen minutes – as obsessively as her son rubs his forehead with that demonic clown's head – she connects with her mother again, maybe for the first time, in a language without words, a language of fear. Her Zoé, ceramic doll, nearly lost in the drips when they come too fast, almost too fast to stop. Her mother is far away, as always, nowhere near her. They will never be close, not like they were in the first flashes of Julie's life, a red ribbon fluttering inside her mother. Her mother is never close, and later, her mother will be mash on the ground, a final fall down, at that moment finally free.

If the three of them are taken away from her – die, vanish, go – she might be free too. Or, if she takes herself away – dies, vanishes, goes – she might set them free. On the back of a flying cat. It makes perfect sense. The three of them on a catamaran flying through indigo waters. She will put it in the section called "Things I Shouldn't Be Capable of Thinking but Am" or, possibly, "Wonders of the World."

VIII

Encounters are contingent. The unique beauty of a perfect encounter is in its chance occurrence. A young girl sits in a corner under a tree and a teacher she has had a crush on for years slides up beside her and whispers, "Stay out of my dreams, kiddo," then moves on, and she knows that fortune has played a distinct role. It's the kind of line that ends careers. The kind of line parents today will tread razors to try to prevent from being thought, let alone uttered. But it happens, despite their best efforts. It happens, one near catastrophe at a time.

The very best encounters are quick as silver, over in a flash, leaving behind a residue of sparks glinting in the late afternoon sun. We wonder, after such encounters, whether they happened at all, trying frantically to trace the logic of their unfolding. He risked everything to tell me I was appearing in his dreams. I was meant to shoulder the blame, apparently, turning up as I was without his permission. I wasn't supposed to be there, and he was choosing this moment beneath a shady tree, under a dusty white sky, to order me to stay away. But in his instruction, how could I not detect the small unruly excess? "Kiddo" signified endearment. "Kiddo" marked his desire for me to return, over and over again. "Kiddo" meant it was an encounter he wanted, despite his strict disavowal. He wanted me in his dreams and, more importantly, he

167

wanted me to know I was already traipsing through them. Unquestionably, he understood that – apart from this exceptional encounter under a tree – there could be nothing more than dreams. Still, even now, I can't deny the pull of that encounter, its imperative beckoning, its excess – that kiddo – frothing over.

~

Snow

Dossiers

I sought to share
the life of snow
and fire.

Adonis, "The Passage"

Charles isn't happy with the shape his ending is taking. He is no longer a young man. He realized this on his fiftieth birthday, his wife, his age, by his side, his few friends, no younger, in view. Looking at them, puffier than he remembered, he knew he had finally crossed the line. He never thought it would happen to him. Rushing like the wind through his thirties and forties, he never thought time would one day arrest. He had assumed it would extend the way it always had for him. No one is that special.

The year Charles turned fifty was the year his father died in his sleep. His father had deserved to die a quiet death after all he had been through, but Charles isn't convinced anyone dies quietly. Failing organs must induce consciousness. Dying bodies surely seek a last glimpse around, one final farewell. Charles can see no possibility of peace in it. The thought of his father awake alone for the last time continues to torment him. Losing his father and turning fifty the same year had not been easy.

It is astonishing to Charles the way trees can withstand the weight of wet snow, the push and pull of the wind. Squirrels and possums scramble to the tips of branches delicate as lace and they will hold. It is coming down to such details, tessellated mosaics in his head. He often sits out on the porch mesmerized, looking at the trees, the half-hidden horizon, the rain, if it is falling, or the snow, blue crystals floating down. He drifts through a passage, a leaf on the wind, till Meredith comes out, splintered with worry and exhaustion, to coax him back inside.

Mere is good, one of the good ones, like his old man. Mere is kind, generous, selfless. Mere is beautiful, still simply lovely with gray hair brushing honey shoulders. Mere notices details, the small things he is only now paying attention to. She pointed these out to him incessantly over the years of their life together, even when they were teenagers and just friends.

Watch for the pink patch under that bird's wing, Charles.

Look at the amethyst light reflecting against that shop window.

Charles, isn't it funny the way kites catch the wind, almost trapping it, and the way the wind slips out from underneath, victorious no matter how long it takes?

Mere charms Charles, though slightly less as the years have accrued. Charm is less important than goodness, however, and it is for her goodness that Charles belongs to Meredith, his wife of thirty-seven years. Meredith and Charles were both twenty when they married, a few months before graduate school. They were going to be teachers. They had known each other in high school, lived in the same neighborhood, were good friends. They hadn't started dating, hadn't fallen in love till college. Charles often wonders why it took so long. Why weren't there flashes of light or extravagant minor chords in the air from the start? At the time, he had convinced himself it was because theirs was an adult relationship, a partnership to raise healthy, confident children. Meredith was good, so incredibly good, and Charles had fallen, without fireworks, for that goodness. But goodness does not transfer. Being with someone good does not make you good. This it would take years for Charles to comprehend.

Charles was nine when his mother died. When he turned twenty-seven he was shocked to think it was the age his mother was when she died. When he turned twenty-nine he was shaken to the roots of his teeth realizing this was the same age his father was when he lost his wife. It scared Charles and it scarred him, though only now is he beginning to recognize how deeply. Charles loves Mere, some years more than others, but he does not love her the way his father loved his mother. He knows this because his father never, not once – despite how ridiculously young he was when his wife died – contemplated remarrying. They were married only ten years. His father said it was enough for a lifetime. His was the kind of love that did not fear loneliness. It was a brave love, a love that could face death standing up. "In her way, she died alone," he would say whenever Charles dared suggest he try to meet someone else. "For her, I will too." And he had, alone in his bed, sleeping soundly, his only son thousands of miles away. The doctor had tried to reassure Charles many times that it was peaceful, that his father had not woken up. Charles remains skeptical.

Charles's life was punctuated by a series of crises, its trajectory propelled by moments of profound misfortune – about one a decade. He wonders whether this is how it is for everyone. The first crisis was the death of his mother when he was nine. Growing up, his father never explained anything. Not till he was twenty-seven could Charles bring himself to ask his father how exactly his mother had died. He suspected cancer because of her hair. Breast cancer, his father confirmed.

Cancer wasn't an illness mentioned much in the late 1950s, certainly not in the suburbs of St. Paul. It was confusing for Charles since his mother seemed fine most of the time. She laughed and made jokes; she cooked for them; she teased his father till his cheeks burned and his lips curled up. But Charles had a dark, hard sense in the space between his ribs and his lungs that things were not quite right. Whispers at night, furtive trips in the late afternoon when he was left with their neighbor, sixty-year-old Mary, who smelled of urine and something else, acrid and cutting, troubled him. Charles hated being left alone with Mary, but he knew to stay quiet, grateful his mother came back that evening or the next day. When his mother's hair began to fall in clumps, he thought nothing of it. Falling hair is not experienced as traumatic if your mother makes it seem normal, which his did. He said nothing, and nothing was said to him, though his mother, toward the end, would hold him tight in her arms at night when she thought he was asleep and breathe in his hair. He would never forget the feel of her cool hand on the back of his neck.

His father worked hard to construct a happy home. He mentioned his wife often so his son would not forget her. He never brought up her illness or her death, but he talked about everything else constantly. He tried as hard as he could to leave the sadness off to one side so Charles would not be burdened by it. Charles was brought up by his father and by the cheerful ghost of his mother. He felt lucky to be cared for by such a good and giving man. Through his childhood and adolescence, he endured silently the hole left in him by his mother's absence, never once mentioning to his old man that a happy phantom couldn't fill it and that memories hurt.

Charles's second crisis came, unsurprisingly, at twenty-seven. What mattered about his second crisis was its outcome. He and Mere were teaching in St. Paul. She taught second grade. He taught seventh and eighth grade science, ninth grade in a pinch. They had been married for seven years. They had been trying to have a baby for seven years. They both wanted children. It was his fault they couldn't. His sperm wasn't quite right. Mere was devastated by the news, as was he. He felt inadequate and small, less of a man. Mere ached for a child, that's how she put it in the early years, before they knew for certain. Once they knew whose fault it was – and he registered the fault as damning – she never mentioned words like "ache" or "desperate" or "yearn" again. She filed such words, along with "family" and "babies," away from herself and from him forever. Her students became her kids. It took him many years to learn to tolerate being around young children. Charles and Mere never considered adoption.

The weight of his mother's lost youth and the regret over his own lost children drove Charles to finalize a decision they had been thinking about for a few years. There were, in the 1970s, many openings to teach at international schools all over the world. One of the reasons Charles and Mere, neither of whom had ever been outside Minnesota, decided to go into teaching in the first place was because they thought it might allow them to travel. Charles's second crisis pushed them to make the break. Apart from occasional visits to Mere's parents and Charles's father, they would not return to the US for twenty-three years. Initially, they planned on Europe – Paris or Frankfurt or Rome – but that didn't seem foreign enough. The Middle East – its sun and dunes together with murky fantasies they both had about tents and camels – beckoned more insistently.

They spent their first four years in Cairo, teaching at the Cairo American College. The following eight years, the longest they every stayed in one place, they taught at the American School of Kuwait. Next, they moved to Pakistan for four years and worked at the International School of Islamabad. They had not expected to stay that long in Pakistan. They figured two years out of the Middle East, for a change, and then back. But their closest friends moved there from Kuwait the year after they did and planned on staying, so Mere and Charles decided to stay too. It was hard to make close friends moving around as much as they did. Veronica and Tom were worth staying for, despite what happened later in Lebanon, the mess he made of their friendship. Their next destination was Abu Dhabi, teaching at the American Community School there. For the last three years of their expatriate life they taught at the American Community School in Beirut. Their final contract was cut short with the news of Charles's father's death. And after Charles's own diagnosis, there was no going back.

The Middle East was infuriating but, to this day, Charles would rather be there than anywhere else in the world. He loved its heat, the weight of its air. He loved the way the light could switch from Mediterranean blue to dull beige or mud brown. Once in Kuwait there was a dust storm that turned the sky maroon, the color of blood let from the slit throat of a goat. The air was still, silent, not gusting the way it usually did during dust storms. The red dust, so many floating atoms, hung in the air. It was exciting to see the sun suspended in the sky, to look at it directly without having to squint, to see it matte, pomegranate-toned, and flat with burnt edges. That happened only once while they were in Kuwait, but there were other storms in other places. He remembered coming upon the pyramids at Giza for the first time through a dust storm so fierce it obliterated the Nile, erased it completely from view. The pyramids and the Sphinx were still there, plopped casually in the desert, the dust behaving the way mist might in Ireland.

Charles coveted every storm the Middle East threw at him.

He also loved the corniches, roads that ran along the shore. There was one in Cairo, Kuwait, Abu Dhabi, and in Beirut. He imagined every Arab country had some version of a corniche. To drive down a corniche in the Middle East with the window down, even in the hell of summer, made him feel invincible. It did something to the lining of his heart, softened it, allowing his chest to expand. It felt like the fulfillment of a silent promise. He had no clue why driving down any road would have this kind of effect on him but it did.

Unlike his fellow expats, Charles was endlessly entertained by all the *bukra inshallah*s. The slapdash, give-me-cash mentality did not repulse him. His sensibilities were simply not that delicate, and he was not so deluded as to believe these traits were exclusively Arab. His colleagues were brought to the edge of madness by the disorganization of the bureaucracy and, worse still, by everyone's shrug-of-the-shoulders attitude. Driver's licenses, health cards, IDs, visas, telephone lines, everything, but everything, would take months and months to obtain, and if you complained you got a glazed stare and the ever ready *bukra inshallah*, tomorrow God-willing. He watched young teachers cry because they had been promised on somebody's father's grave their phone line would be functional the following day. They had been looked in the eye and sworn to that it would work. It never did. Not the following day, not the day after, and not the day after that. Not until some gears were greased would that phone line crackle to life. None of this fazed Charles. It grounded him. It made him feel safe.

Now, at fifty-seven, he is far from grounded. He is unraveling or already unraveled. There are the little details he picks out daily. Those help. He counts them one by one, the way old men at outdoor cafés in Cairo or Beirut worry their beads or the way he used to count his marbles when he was a little boy. Most of the time, though, he feels like he is being lowered into an icy lake. He feels his toes go in, then his ankles and calves up to his knees. He hangs there for a bit, the blood in his feet and lower legs thickening. After about a minute or so, he is lowered again, half his torso in the frozen water, his extremities mercifully numb and brittle. He is plunged in quickly after that, the frigid water closing over his heavy head with a swoosh. He never struggles, his body a bag of stones. He welcomes the pricking fire of the water. None of this means Charles wants to die. He is certain he doesn't want that yet, not for a while. There are still the details to collect and the layers of memory to archive.

What does one teacher matter? In particular, what is the weight in worth of a childless teacher, a man not always good? Not much, he is beginning to figure. When the young pharmacist with the blue-black hair hands him his orange plastic cylinder of pills, presents them to him with an unsolicited smile, it brings him to tears. It is one of the details he counts. Though her smile to him is probably genuine, what does it disclose about his value to the world? Not a thing.

He has done wrong in his life, and it weighs heavy on him, makes it excruciating to be alone. He is not a bad man. He did not, for instance, practice the inveterate evil of a serial killer. He just isn't good, not the way Mere is, not the way his father had been. At the time, he hadn't lost any sleep over it. What had he done? He had slept with a number of women other than his wife. Ten other women. If Mere had left him when he was in his forties, he would have recovered. He would have felt lonely for a while, but he would have still been young enough to believe something else was possible, that a different breed of passion was attainable with a different woman for a different version of a lifetime. He knows now, especially in his state, it is too late. Who would want him, old man before his time? Mere is a saint for staying, for loving him despite his behavior, which she knew all about, which he never (except for that one shameful encounter under a tree he would take

179

with him to his grave) tried to hide from her. What kind of woman would put up with what he had done? Even now he isn't sure why she is still here, not that he is ungrateful. He is grateful every day, so grateful it makes his heart as limp as his dick.

For twenty years he was sexually faithful to Meredith, the first woman he ever slept with. Being faithful wasn't difficult in his twenties. He loved Mere and wanted to start a family with her. During those early years, his genuine feelings for his wife and his intense longing for kids kept him committed. It was the best he ever was. After learning he was sterile, Charles's libido froze. He would try to satisfy Mere, but he was clumsy and self-conscious. He wanted neither her nor anyone else. His dead desire kept Charles loyal to his wife through his thirties.

In his forties, he strayed. It was the usual, nothing in the least exceptional. It was the same ugly shape of anyone's indiscretion. He slept with women much less attractive, much less intelligent, much less generous, much less than Mere. With these women he had the kind of sex he felt he couldn't with his wife. He would bend their bodies over. He would knead them into a shape, long and sinewy, that could wrap around his anger and strangle it. Until he turned forty he hadn't fully grasped the vastness of his anger. He had acknowledged his sorrow over the broken lives of his parents, his anguish over his missing children, but he had not recognized his anger. His affairs were packed with it, and it made the sex burn. What he came to realize over the years, as the rage slowly diminished, was that his affairs were as much about fear as they were anger. He fucked women who meant nothing to him because he was afraid of getting older. More precisely, he was afraid of getting older with a woman he loved without fervor, and he was afraid of getting older bereft, as he was, of offspring. He could not tolerate the idea of his mother's genes coming to an end. He would be explaining to his students about DNA and RNA, about the passing on of genes, dominant or recessive, and he would suddenly feel on the brink of collapse. He would stand quietly in his place, as still as possible, trying to fight the urge to pull his hair out of his head or scrape the skin off his face or puncture the backs of his knees with a sharpened pencil, anything to erase the overwhelming realization that would smack him as if for the first time, though it was the hundredth, the thousandth time. Without children of his own, his mother's death was irreversible. The only thing that would hold back his imminent collapse in the middle of class, in front of twenty-five thirteen-year-olds, was the thought of pushing whomever she happened to be that year against a wall and filling her with his wretched semen.

Charles made it a point not to sleep with women he worked with, and of the ten, nine were strangers to his wife. He was honest with Mere about his affairs from the start. He hid nothing, though he did not believe this absolved him of anything. In fact, he realized it may have been worse of him to tell her than to hide it from her. Hiding it, at least, showed some respect. He thought of those French or Italian husbands venerating their wives, protecting them from their transgressions. There was no need to bring them into it. It usually passed like indigestion. Why destroy everything in the process? The difference between Charles and those impeccable

Casanovas was the children, the spectacular silhouette of a family worth preserving, worth lying for. Confessing to Mere was an act of selfishness. He must have wanted to hurt her, to punish her for something. She would have found out on her own – ten years of infidelity is a long time, with many occasions to discover misdeeds. For her to have found out on her own would have given her power. It might have impelled her to leave him, to look for someone worthy of her. He didn't want to take that risk, so he told her right from the start. He spared her the specifics, but he told her with whom and generally when. He was a coward.

There was another reason Charles fucked around, apart from sorrow, anger, and fear. He did it for exuberance. Exuberance: energy, excitement, luxuriant growth, even, at its root, fruitfulness. He cheated because, as he was doing it, even as he was thinking about doing it, it made him believe something tremendous might happen. It gave him the sense that there was time for everything, no end in sight. It felt like holding a small hand in his or watching light laddered through blinds. Doing what he knew he shouldn't be brought him life in a crystal bowl. It had been taken away too early in a scream of late night sirens and a speeding ambulance. He was reclaiming it. All wrong he was going about doing it, but he was trying. There was exposure in those meaningless encounters, a stripping away. It was not about revealing himself to the women, and it was most certainly not about the women revealing anything about themselves to him. He was not in the least interested in that form of exchange. What was revealed to Charles, what was exposed to him every time he slept with a woman not his wife, was another seed of potential. Nothing else generated the same charge of electricity beneath the surface of his skin. Exuberance, the luxurious fruit of possibility. It was his addiction.

Charles never experienced the waves of potential in his teens and twenties that most young people take for granted. There they were, stomping through yellow leaves as crunchy as Cheerios, huddling together in a corner of the library late into the night, experiencing collectively the deviant ecstasy of a snow day, and he felt apart. He could see their lives, endlessly open, precious, but not his own. He existed in a detached bubble, confounded by the simplest choices, making selections as though from miles away, as though for someone else. It wasn't until his early thirties, with one of his students, that he got a taste of what he had been missing. He is so ashamed to think of it, even now, decades later, when what could any of it possibly matter? It makes him hang his head. If only he could smother the shame and live with that first taste of exuberance. If only he could clear a space, tiny, secret (nobody has to know), inside himself so he could relive it a hundred times, over and over again until he is dead. He seeks that early purity. Back to a time before he knew what it would become, before he knew what the need for it would make him do. He wants again what Mina made him feel for the first time when he was thirty-two.

Mere helps him up, holds his arm firmly as he walks to the couch. He doesn't need her help, he hardly sways, but he lets her give it to him. A few months ago he would not have survived without her help. He is stronger now. He can walk into the pharmacy on his own, fix himself a sandwich, wrap the covers around his own shoulders. But Meredith lives – even after every appalling thing he has done – for him. She seems to want to do nothing but administer to his needs. Pills, warmth, nutrition, bathroom. Why? She is healthy, full of energy, still lovely, her gray hair mesmerizing. Why is Mere suspending her own life for his? It is heavy, much too heavy to die carrying.

Charles is dying. He has testicular cancer. They have removed what they can. They claim the odds are in his favor. Charles doesn't believe them. He knows he is dying. Poetic justice. He is not a brave man. He is not like his mother. He is not like his father. He does not want to die, but neither does he want to fight. It is a conundrum. He wants to live in order to go backwards, to curl back into the spaces of exuberance, to chronicle those moments, each and every one. His present is over and he cares nothing about his future. He wants to live only so he can organize a series of dossiers with colored labels documenting everything. He won't write down what happened. What happened isn't what matters. That's why Charles always told Mere about his affairs. She was routinely kept abreast of what was happening. What truly matters, however, he has never shared. What matters is precisely what he wants to file away.

He kept things in the course of his affairs. He collected oddments and slight objects from his lovers, things they would never miss. Grocery lists, shopping receipts, tickets for various performances, pages from magazines or books they happened to be reading, postcards or junk they may have received in the mail, balled-up tissues, chewed-up straws or toothpicks or pencils, the crust off their toast, colored hair bands and clips, candy wrappers, instructions for their husbands left on fridge doors, tags from their clothes, lint from under their beds, cigarette butts stamped with their lipstick, strands of their hair, feathers or fur from their pets, flowers from their gardens. He wants to arrange these scraps in files. He wants to shape together the impossible logic of his forties, to put together the dots otherwise scattered every which way. He isn't looking for sense, nor is he seeking closure. All he wants is a way back to Mina.

He met Mina his second year in Kuwait. She was in his seventh grade science class. She was twelve years old and a stunner. He recognized in a naked instant his admiration was not innocent. This was new. He recoiled automatically, his stomach duly bruised. But something else began to spread open at the same time, something that made him feel stupendous, puffing fast and huge with expectation. He had never had this particular sensation before, this desert of intensity. There was a pointy rebellion inside, and he found it impossible to speak, to welcome that year's seventh graders to life science, where they were going to learn about the building blocks of life – cells, plants, animals, humans – all rolled up together in the busy reproductive fabric called existence. Something in him was being choked, and he didn't want the marvel of that asphyxiation to stop because it was unclogging another tributary, one he had no idea ran through him.

Mina's body was a tendril. Her eyes, dark pools of intelligence, made her look thirty and her voice was surprisingly deep. When she spoke in class, it took every ounce of control to stop himself from touching her face. Ruin was on the horizon, but for the first time in his life, he felt free from the threat of impending catastrophe. The best thing about Mina in the seventh grade was that she had absolutely no sense of her own flawlessness. She carried her immaculate beauty around like something she could afford to lose. It was exactly this Charles found irresistible, what he wanted to possess until the end of the world.

He taught her in the seventh grade. He was nice to her, favored her, though he was always discreet. He left the door of his classroom open during lunch time and announced to his classes that students were free to come in if it was too hot outside. He knew the boys never would – there were marbles, footballs, computer games outside. Most of the girls didn't either. Mina and two or three of her friends were regulars though. He would pretend to be busy with his preparations for class. He would sit calmly at the front of the room, papers and books spread before him, patiently counting chunks of time – five minutes, ten, fifteen – then, and not every day, he would allow himself a glimpse. He would not move his head at all. He moved only his eyes, up or to the left or right, to Mina. About midway through the year, Mina began to come to him. She told him things, her voice hesitant but conveying a confidence she shouldn't have had at that age. He let her talk to him about her crushes, about how her legs hurt at night, about the music she liked. She would shove her Walkman at him, laugh at his inept bobbing to an unfamiliar beat. She would come in close as he listened. He would be able to recognize her smell in a dark room, even now. She smelled like snow or the sun in winter or smoke from fire on a freezing night. She smelled like weather he had known as a boy, which confused him. She was a whirlwind of joy with a serene center.

The following year he didn't teach Mina science, but she still came to visit him during her breaks. At thirteen, she was beginning to understand what her body could do. She flirted with Charles mercilessly, and he played the fool. His obsession with her pushed him to extremes. From extremes of happiness – a roiling delirium that took him into the desert on weekends to stare gratefully at an indigo sky and a galloping moon – to extremes of sorrow – a tormented lament for the lives he would never lead because he had grown up without a mother, because he would never have children of his own. His lows left Meredith bewildered. He was inconsolable. His hollow moans escaped from under the locked bathroom door, but to his wife's concerned queries he was resistant as tarp.

The year after that, his fourth year in Kuwait, Charles arranged with the school to teach ninth grade biology. He didn't like teaching high schoolers, especially not high school boys, but he wanted Mina in his classroom one last time. He needed to see her every day. He was ashamed of himself, the things he was thinking about her. There was a steady build up of danger, danger all around. He was jumping into a volcano of folly, there was no stopping him. His dreams were taking over his waking life. She was there every night. When he saw her the next morning, biology class came first, she seemed impossibly familiar. None of it made sense to him. Three years was a long time. He convinced himself it could not be a simple fixation. This was love. She was young, but he imagined waiting for her to get older, waiting for her to graduate from college so that he could marry her. He would have children with her – it wasn't his fault after all. With her, everything, every possible life, could materialize. He was positive, certain he loved her, would love her always.

When she turned fifteen, in the tenth grade, Mina pulled away from him. In any case, that's what it felt like to him. He hardly ever saw her. He caught slivers of her – waves, cheery smiles, hellos light as air. She was elsewhere. Her life still unfurling. She was flying high. For Charles, it was ending. Exuberance was collapsing, after only three years. He wanted more.

He saw her one December day sitting silent under a tree. It was rare to see Mina by herself, her still center always attracting others as it did, fine young boys he could never hope to compete with, their own lives expanding as robustly as hers. That early afternoon, though, she was alone under the low branches of a tree. He slid up to her without thinking, so close he could smell her once again, that same snow smell he wanted to scoop up. This was it. He stared into her eyes like he had never done before, inhaled her into his very soul, brought his mouth to her ear – this was going to get him fired, he knew it would, but he was in the midst of folly and there were no brakes underfoot – and whispered, "Stay out of my dreams, kiddo." He had never and would never again use that word. "Kiddo" should have been reserved for his own kids. "Kiddo" would have pushed him to break the knees of any man saying it to his own daughter. That whispered "kiddo" under the tree was the death of his exuberance. Kiddo, for whom every fuck in his forties had been and for whom now, inexplicably, he wants to put together endless files, a labyrinth of dossiers through which he might trace his way back to what she had made him feel all those years ago, to her smell.

It took Charles four years after the encounter under the tree to put Mina on the back burner and to acknowledge exuberance, his for so short a time, was gone forever. Turning forty helped him rediscover his desire for sex. He slept with Mere, he slept with others, and he found an unconventional balance for about a decade.

Their last year abroad was in Beirut. They had been there for two years, were crazy about it, and signed a second two-year contract. Charles felt he might be coming out of his haze and, for several months, started nothing new with anyone. Once again, their friends Veronica and Tom had ended up in the same place as them. They had been friends for almost fifteen years. They too were childless. Veronica's fault. This brought them all closer together since most of their colleagues, if they weren't too young, had children and always socialized with their children, which neither Charles nor Tom could take. Charles loved Tom, the only man besides his father he loved with an open heart. Tom knew about Charles's affairs. He was a man without judgment, and he was gentle with his friend. Midway through their third year in Beirut, Charles turned fifty. Tom and Veronica were there for his birthday.

Charles wasn't just anticipating a midlife crisis, he was staging it himself. They all got very drunk that night. Charles followed Veronica into a room. He held her by the wrists and pushed her against a ready wall. He kissed her and she responded at first. He pushed harder and she started to resist. He could see himself, his bloated stomach and already sagging thighs. It was farcical and he could hear her saying no. He continued anyway and Tom walked through the door. There were tears and screams and rage. There were ugly accusations and a destroyed friendship. He had violated Veronica. There could be no future for him. Mere did not speak to him until the phone call with the news about his father four months later. Mere did not speak to him but, as always, Mere stayed.

It isn't forgiveness he is after. It isn't redemption, either. He has paid his dues, living longer than his mother had, not holding his father in his arms as he lay dying in a lonely bed. He lives in a world where oil could burn hot enough to turn the sky black at noon, the sun a slate circle in the sky. A place where people die by the hundreds in the desert, throats slashed, villages purged. A place where bodies are blown to bits by other bodies blowing up. What could he possibly matter in the middle of all that? Forgiveness? Redemption? His life isn't history, but it is in ruins. He has fathered no one. There is no going forward. But there is a way back. Onward he will die, backward he will find his way. Through the small things his wife has known about all along (the beads those old men counted, the marbles of his childhood, the mosaics in his head), he hopes to wend his way back.

Meredith holds out her hand to him, and he takes it. He will hold it tight enough to get through. Holding her hand and counting the beads, the marbles, the smallest, unsolicited smiles, the tears in his eyes, he will get through. A passage through the dossiers. For a life of snow. For goodness unfurling, taking him in.

IX

Elsa was a Christian Iraqi. Her parents were firecracker smart. They realized early on that they couldn't remain in Iraq and that Kuwait, pleasant as it was at the time, wouldn't last. They left to the US in the early 1970s, stayed for the time required to get a green card, and then returned to Kuwait for another decade to earn enough money to build their dream home in Georgia. I remember Elsa in the third grade, braided hair in hoops around her ears, starched white collar under her sharply ironed navy blue jumper. Elsa spewed a million words a minute, conclusions I always believed, like I would a teacher's or a mother's. She was my age, but she felt like my big sister. One year, Elsa told me her aunt was dying of cancer and that she was going to become a doctor when she grew up so she could find a cure. I had no idea what she was talking about, but I had no doubt she would do it. (I wish, Elsa, you had found the cure. You promised, Elsa, and I believed you.)

Over the years, I learned to trust her completely when it came to the things that mattered – a yellow, yes, yellow sweater went best with my favorite gray pleated skirt; I was, for goodness sake, thin enough; my taste in New Wave, highly cultivated, was impeccable; kissing two boys in a week certainly did not make anyone a slut.

Elsa lived in a wonderland apartment complex. It had a huge pool in the middle and you could smell the sea

191

nearby. The families who lived there – from Palestine, Iraq, Egypt, assorted European countries, the US – all had kids who went either to the same school we did or to one of the other familiar internationals. Neighbors did not leave their smelly shoes outside their doors. Children did not thump and scream all day and night like irredeemable demons. There was football out front, marble-clad pillars marking goal posts. There were bikinis on lounge chairs, mothers no older than we are now smoking slowly, eyeing their children through oversized sunglasses. A slumber party at Elsa's was a weekend affair that started after school on Wednesday, involved a night at the ice rink, a lazy Thursday afternoon by the pool – scoping the boys scoping us – a party in the evening, and concluded on Friday afternoon, warm as soup. Those vanished weekends still make perfect sense, like a parallelogram or a Polaroid picture.

~

Amerika's

Box

The decision to change their five-year-old daughter's name was a bold one for Ahmed and Fatma to make. Kuwait was, after all, a country tangled in red tape. But like most of their fellow citizens in the year 1991, Ahmed and Fatma wanted to commemorate their nation's gratitude to America. Fatma was in her late forties. It had been a few years since she was last pregnant. They knew something drastic had to be done, so they ploughed patiently through daunting name change procedures. They submitted pillars of forms to the proper ministries. Small bundles of cash slipped quietly under desks. They publicized their young daughter's new name in two newspapers. Once the paperwork was done, Ahmed and Fatma informed friends and family of the change and invited everyone to their home to celebrate over *istikan*s of saffron tea. Men in one room, women in the other, eating like locusts and singing along to music. They were free once again, safe together in the long afternoon.

Ahmed and Fatma were not wealthy. They lived in government housing near a gas station in the city center. Ahmed pushed paper in a ministry job that masked unemployment. Fatma stayed at home, swamped with the details of domesticity. Their decision to have eight children was largely economic. While both had an uneasy sense that birth control, like a gynecological exam, was against Islam, it was mostly for the per-child social allowance that they had permitted their family to grow. Each newborn added fifty dinars a month to Ahmed's paltry salary. Fifty times eight could not be passed up, so Fatma had spent most of her adult life ballooned by babies.

With every pregnancy, Fatma prayed for a girl. A daughter to follow in her footsteps and to help with chores. A daughter to share the burden of her disappointments, to scold and to love. A daughter to plan a wedding for, to take care of her and her husband in their old age. None of the first seven pregnancies answered her prayers. By the eighth she had stopped asking, accepting that the girls she would choose for her sons to marry would be as close to daughters as she was going to get. Her baby girl's unasked for arrival was, to Fatma, a sign of Allah's subtle endorsement of her years of *du'aa*. To Ahmed, his daughter was, more simply, a reason to soften, a way to escape the noose of habit.

Young Amerika Ahmed Al-Ahmed took to her new name instantly. The oily gray man in charge of stamping name change forms had mistakenly replaced the *c* in America with a *k*. He had picked up snippets of English here and there, and America sounded to him like it should have a *k* in it. In any case, he was starving and wanted to leave work early for lunch. He had no time to look into trivialities. By the time Ahmed was informed by the oily gray man in charge of receiving name change forms that America was spelled with a *c* not a *k*, it was too late. If Ahmed wanted to change that single letter, he would have to wait until after the weekend and pray for the unlikelihood that both oily gray men showed up for work. Ahmed made the wise decision to accept the *k*; it didn't really matter since his daughter's name would be written mostly in Arabic. As it turned out, Amerika would come to love her accidental *k* especially. A *k* like a kick in the air, like a Radio City Rockette.

In elementary school, Amerika felt special. Nobody else had her name. She didn't know what exactly America was then. All she knew was that whenever she told people her name it made them exuberant. "Yes! We should be grateful. If it weren't for America, we would be part of Iraq, *Allah la yagooleh*. You will never forget to be thankful to America. Neither should we." Always the exuberance. To begin with.

The only person in those early years who responded differently to Amerika's name was her religion teacher. *Abla* Nada was tightly wound, a pinprick of a woman, with a face as thick as coffee. Her head was securely bandaged in black, a *hijab* covering her hair, her forehead down to her eyebrows, half her cheeks, and most of her chin. As she spoke, her saliva sprayed onto open books, shiny desks, the tops of students' heads, the blackboard. "An infelicitous name for an infelicitous little girl. You are doomed, my dear. With a name like that, there will be no redemption for you. Nor for any of us who dare to step across Allah's line. In your graves, you all will hear the footsteps of your mourners walking away, leaving you alone. Your punishment will begin as your grave starts to shrink around you and you feel the hot breath of hell encircle your body, you smell its rot, its pus, its blood and urine." Saucer-eyed children listened in terror, unable to close their ears or their hearts to her words. Only Amerika seemed immune. She listened to *Abla* Nada's tales of torture and punishment like she would ghost stories around a campfire. She scooped up her teacher's chatter as she did her grandmother's about what it was like to grow up in the desert, about how the skies used to be a shattering blue that reminded you to be grateful for beauty and birds. *Abla* Nada's accounts were stories and Amerika loved stories. Her friends left class trembling, crying, promising to pray. Amerika left with a kick of the heels, a Rockette, a rocket, the letter *k* in search of adventure.

Amerika pronounced her name "Amreeka," with a stress on the *r* not the *m*, because that's how America is pronounced in Arabic. She had no idea that it was pronounced differently in other places, at least not till she was about seven and started watching satellite TV. Then she learned it could also be pronounced "Ammurrika" or "Amereek." She discovered her name was a place, a big place with tall buildings and wide open spaces and violent storms with lots of rain and snow. She learned about icicles that clung to the branches of trees like crystal fingers. About trees with leaves that changed color, bursting into orange and red, yellow ocher and chestnut brown. She found out about Halloween and dressing up in scary costumes. She thought *Abla* Nada might enjoy the idea of Halloween, obsessed as she was with the shape and smell of death, but *Abla* Nada told Amerika in no uncertain terms that she would be sent straight to hell simply for knowing about such things. Amerika retorted that if hell was anything like Halloween, full of trick-or-treating and jack-o'-lanterns, she would gladly go.

Amerika learned about baseball, hitting a white ball with a stick and running and spitting on the ground. About Babe Ruth, left-handed hero. About cowboys and horses, mother-of-pearl buttons on flower-embroidered, close-fitting shirts. About skies like fields that turned yellow and green before a storm, clouds that colored the mountains black and blue, and funnels that came down and destroyed hundreds of homes, decimated lives and left sad old photographs floating in the aftermath, carried by a remnant wind.

Amerika discovered New York City, a cathedral of a place, gray and glittery, with a park in the middle of it, a lake in the middle of the park, and a woman standing tall in the ocean. Everything exciting happened in New York. It was a maze of crime and food sold on street corners. It had numbered avenues with square intersections and yellow taxicabs. Intersections in Kuwait were round, taxis orange. Manhattan was an island, like the Kuwaiti island of Failaka, though, unlike Failaka, Alexander the Great had never been there. Alexander had named Failaka "Icarus," after a son who flew too close to the sun.

The grandest thing Amerika learned was the language. Not just English . . . *American*. She rolled her tongue around its *r*s like a parrot, owned its nasal crescendos and punchy confidence. American pried opened a world of wonder for Amerika.

Watching American television via satellite over the years, Amerika came to believe people laughed more in that vast place that stretched further than it seemed possible to stretch – from sea to shining sea. To contain this vastness, this remarkable joy, to make it hers, Amerika decided when she was ten

199

to keep a box, to fill it with as much of America as she possibly could. Amerika knew she had the propensity to collect like a magpie, so she decided to limit the size of her box. A wooden box, about ten inches squared, with a hinged lid. Inside, the box was divided into twenty-five compartments, each two inches by two inches. She had insisted on going to see the carpenter herself, to the amusement of both the carpenter and her father. She didn't want the box to be too heavy, but it had to be sturdy. The lid was to have a lock in the middle and the key had to be made of brass.

Designing the box was the easy part. Figuring out what twenty-five objects to put into the box was much harder, and they would vary over the years. At ten, Amerika filled her compartments with: the wrapper of a Baby Ruth bar (her uncle had brought her back a bag of candy from Florida); green jellybeans; grape Bubble Yum; five different colored cat's-eye marbles (she had seen television kids in a schoolyard flicking them during recess); a small American flag on a toothpick; a clam shell (for clambakes); a wooden Santa; peanuts (for peanut butter, which, she learned, should be eaten on soft white Wonder Bread with the crusts cut off and strawberry or grape jelly not jam); a folded page ripped out of an *Archie* comic; a teensy teepee she got out of a Kinder Egg (not sold in America but usually containing stuff to do with America); a John Wetteland baseball card (1996 World Series MVP); an Elvis pin; an orange maple leaf cut out of felt; a short string of popcorn; Fruit Loops (she loved the curve and stretch of the word "loop"); an Abraham Lincoln penny; a yellow HB2 wood pencil (sharpened down to almost nothing, pink eraser intact); a small silver figurine of the Empire State Building; a Coke bottle cap; a McDonald's cheeseburger wrapper (after liberation, the biggest McDonald's in the world rose like a neon castle on the Gulf Road); a foot of dental floss; a falcon's feather as a stand-in for a bald eagle's (brought back from the brink of extinction, symbol of national pride); a Fisher Price Little People pilot with a round brown head on a blue plastic body (finding out about slavery would rupture somewhat Amerika's faith in American joy); and a Winnie-the-Pooh sticker. Amerika filled the final compartment on the lower right hand corner with American idioms written neatly on strips and scraps of paper. She wrote with tiny handwriting so that she could fit as many as possible in the two-by-two space:

Acapulco gold

ass in a sling

at first blush

between the devil and the deep blue sea

by the seat of one's pants

cock-and-bull story

fat of the land

flat as a pancake

for Pete's sake

get down to brass tacks

hard as nails

Indian summer

in the twinkling of an eye

into thin air

laughed my head off

lickety-split

lit up like a Christmas tree

lump in my throat

many moons ago

out of the blue

paint the town red

pooped out

scream bloody murder

sell snow to the Eskimos

square peg in a round hole

stars in your eyes

under my skin

the world is your oyster

zip it

This compartment was Amerika's favorite, and it was always stuffed to capacity. She had decided at the very beginning that whatever came out of the box had to be thrown away before a new object was added, but she couldn't bring herself to throw away the idioms. If she wanted to add a new idiom to an already full compartment, she would carefully choose one to remove. The only condition she set herself was that the first letter of the removed idiom had to match the first letter of the idiom to be newly inserted. So, for example, if she wanted to add "mad as a hornet" to a full compartment, "many moons ago" had to be removed. Once retired, old idioms, organized alphabetically, were placed in a great black stamp album that looked like a witch's spell book. Amerika liked the crinkling sound of the white protective tissues between the heavy pages. She adored the way her scraps looked, odd sizes and textures, splayed against the black. She would come to love that book almost more than the box.

Amerika never took her box with her to school, though she spent most of her time there thinking about it. School had become a nightmare for Amerika. The gulf between her life at home, comfortably padded with satellite TV and, soon enough, the Internet, and her life at school, where teachers like *Abla* Nada were multiplying like spiders, was becoming intolerable. Because she was the youngest, the most cherished, the long-awaited, her parents left her to her own devices. They were impressed with her sponging up of English – "Not just any English," she would boast to them, "*American* English!" – with her ability to entertain herself for hours, and with her commitment to her special projects, baffling as these sometimes were to them.

Amerika loved to read. Nobody in her family ever picked up a book if they didn't have to, and they never had to. The idea of reading a novel or poetry or anything other than the newspaper wouldn't have occurred to them. Amerika didn't learn the habit at school either. Students were discouraged from reading anything other than the Qur'an. But Amerika felt instinctively that reading was a chance to imagine new worlds in words. It was a way to create chinks in walls where they weren't supposed to be. She had figured out on her own that the only way she was really going to learn English was by reading books in the language. She loved Beverly Cleary, Louise Fitzhugh, Judy Blume. She saw herself in Harriet the Spy, Sheila the Great, and Nancy Drew. She begged her older brothers to drive her again and again to the Family Bookshop in Salmiya. They always did.

Amerika's seven older brothers didn't want to impose their will upon their little sister. She was delightful in her smallness, a jack-in-the-box in the middle of their nothing-special lives. They teased her about her America obsession, about her book fixation, about being a girl and being the youngest, but they did not tell her what to do or what to think. She knew, from stories friends told her about their own brothers, that hers were exceptional. At first her mother had wanted to mold her daughter, the way she had been molded by her mother, into a baby-making shape that could balloon and grow but not fly into the sky like a bird or a kite. But Fatma quickly decided she would rather Amerika take shape on her own and make her own shapes in turn. Maybe it was because she was her only daughter, her final child in a line of children, the one she hadn't prayed for but who had answered her prayers. Fatma was taking a risk, making a quiet decision to allow something she could not predict to happen. Amerika was as grateful as honey for her mother's arms around her, for her brothers, for her Mr. Rogers in a *dishdasha* father, for the way things were at home. It made her life at school tolerable, but only just.

By the time Amerika turned fourteen, every single girl in her class at the all-girls government school was a *mutahajiba*. Their heads were covered up, swaddled, one by one. A child would pop her newly wrapped head into the classroom and all the other girls would rush over to kiss and congratulate her, to ask what had made her come to her senses. "I dreamed of a serpent coiled around my thighs and felt its teeth sinking into my skin. I woke up crying, and my mother said it was Allah's way of reminding me that my uncovered hair was a sin. She's right. It's my turn." Many of the girls didn't have a choice. At ten or eleven their parents forced them to wear the veil, their little heads covered in darkness, their mermaid hair out of the light forever. Some girls covered up because everyone else was doing it. They gave in to the pressure like television teenagers gave in to smoking in bathrooms or unprotected sex. Others did it because they believed it would pave the way for marriage. They imagined dark eyes appreciatively surveying the iconic bit of cloth. These girls glided through the air, their pert bodies draped in multicolored chiffons sparkling with sequins. Still others, with the sharp cheddar fervor of true believers, covered their entire faces in black, a new, creepier breed of *niqab*. And the *niqab* – permitting only sullen eyes to peep through curtains of black – was suddenly everywhere.

Amerika's mother told her that before the invasion *munaqqaba*s were rare. They could be found mainly around the outskirts of the city or in the desert where the Bedouins lived. "But after liberation, *ya habibti*, Kuwaitis seem to have caught the virus." Amerika's mother wore a black *abaya* like a magician's cape around her shoulders when she went to the *souk* or to visit friends. She was not veiled because she said it was not the old Kuwaiti way, at least not the way it was when she was growing up. "Kuwaiti women were modest but they were not mice, Amerika. We were never mice." Amerika would jump up and down on her mother's bed and yell, "We are not mice! We are not mice! I am not a mouse! I REFUSE TO BE A MOUSE!" Amerika's hair was as lovely as her mother's, rich mahogany waves lapping her shoulders. There was no way she was ever going to cover it up. Her hair was her. It was her mother's loop of love flowing, and she refused to hide it away.

Amerika's obstinacy meant she had to deal every day with the acid gaze of teachers and the cruelty of classmates. Suffering years of their relentless pestering was draining, sometimes almost more than Amerika could bear. She put up with it because she knew in four years it would all come to an end. In four years she would finish secondary school and go to university. She would be the first in her family to do so. She would study English literature and it would set her free. That dream, along with satellite TV and her beloved books, kept Amerika going. She would have wanted her teenage years to mirror Betty and Veronica's. Going to the movies on a date, pool parties and bonfires on the beach, spin the bottle and first base, chili fries and root beer floats with her best friends forever on Saturday afternoons. She would have wanted the Macy's Day Parade and touch football on a nippy fall day. Footloose and fancy free, fun in the sun, and the devil take the hindmost. That would never be hers. Still, she knew she had more than most, so she put up with her solitude and with the bitterness of others. She put up with it because she had her box to put it into.

Amerika's box was for the extras, for the not quite rights but the wanting it anyways. Every desire to and yearning for was there. Some objects remained in compartments for months, even years. In other compartments there was a tornado of changes. From a red Lifesaver, to a snippet of jeans, to a cherry-flavored condom virtually overnight. She played her box like a virtuoso musician, fingers flying across compartments, folding, unfolding, arranging, rearranging,

206

sliding in, pulling out, ceaselessly. She spent hours hunched over it, examining it from every angle, carefully considering what belonged beside what and for how long. The hours of the day she was away from it, she was thinking about it, drawing maps, making lists. Her maps looked like constellation charts, her lists like clever haikus. Amerika's box was her escape, her window opening when the doors, one by one, were clicking shut.

When the buildings came down, everything changed. Suddenly it was no longer Amerika and America together. Now it was the Axis of Evil and terror under every rock; it was us and them and never the two shall meet. Amerika was, lickety-split, completely alone. Her name, no longer exuberance to others, often triggered fury and furrowed brows. Her box had been her portal to elsewhere, her string of idioms a fishing line to an alternative pond, bigger and better. Instead of marriage and children, instead of a dead-end job at a ministry or bank, instead of segregated tea parties, her box and her album were travel and ambition, optimism and go-getting, mountain climbing and paragliding. But after the buildings came down, Amerika slowly turned into a half-knit sweater unraveling. She started to come undone like the laces of bright white Converse hi-tops. To stop the weighted stones, the magnet pull, Amerika began to collect buttons for the compartment where three Tootsie Rolls used to be. Ghost white buttons. Misty rose and dim gray buttons. Firebrick red and burnt sienna buttons. Buttons of pale flesh. Buttons for empty spaces, for something missing, for reaching outward and spreading she wasn't quite sure what or where to anymore.

Her search for the right color buttons held things in check for a while, through secondary school, until she turned seventeen and heard about the ring of fire around Baghdad.

Iraq was the other side of Amerika. It was as much for Iraq as for America that Amerika was named, though in a different direction, away from rather than toward, despite rather than because of. Growing up, she hadn't given much thought to Iraq, to Iraqis. Saddam Hussein was the bogeyman lurking under the bed with spindly green fingers waiting to grab unsuspecting ankles. But Saddam was not death to Amerika. He was no longer a threat, no longer armies marching in, tanks rolling down the Fifth Ring Road, hellfires burning. He was no longer bullets in brains and homes gutted, at least not for Amerika. She didn't know Saddam had made her father cry for the first time in his adult life, had made her mother get down on creaky knees to take her husband's head in her hands, to smooth away foreign tears, to knead hard the strangeness of being taken over, gulped up in a day. Ahmed and Fatma wanted to spare her, their little sprout, the memory of loss, the skeleton of fear. But it was in her name, hollered impatiently, whispered with concern. Iraq was in Amerika. Saddam was there. Fear was there. Her name was the maze of memory, an ant threading a shell, around and around. It was loss – deep, sharp cuts into the bodies of fish, waxy feathers melting in the sun.

Amerika had always felt her life unfolding like her box. Amerika was a virgin but she didn't want to be. She wanted to feel herself glistening and unfolding in someone's arms. When she thought about sex, she saw herself in an airplane or at an airport. She saw LAX or JFK or O'Hare, sometimes even Fiumicino or Charles de Gaulle. She saw her box in her arms and a JanSport slung across her back. When Amerika thought about her box, she felt her body free, uncovered. She dreamed of belonging to herself, of being alone and not being afraid to be alone. She imagined what it would feel like to glow. At seventeen, Amerika was ready for something to happen to her, to her body, to her box. When she felt herself being pushed into the Axis of Evil, into the center of its wicked triangle, despised, spat upon, after all this time, she made the decision to wait. This was not her moment. She forced her body to recoil back into its shell, no ant circling and threading with ingenuity, with care. She stopped anticipating the smell of the Atlantic. She had begun to see in America her direction home, from sea to shining sea. But it was spitting her out now. She had to pause it all, to stop before everything came undone, before it all unraveled to nothing. Amerika waited with bated breath.

Then the war came. Not her war exactly. Not her country's war. Not exactly, but inexactly it was hers, her country's too. Here it was, the stones weighing down, and her body, pure as the moment before flight, never to be her own. Kuwaitis were told to stay inside, to seal the windows with duct tape and plastic; it was too late for gas masks. There would be a symphony of sirens, a swell of sound, and then a mad scramble into the safe room, sweating, gasping, thirsty. Dodging Scuds for America, Scuds from Iraq. Once, twice, three times Amerika and her family scrambled, crammed together like dates in a crate, and then her father, Ahmed, decided to ignore the wailing, to stay put because he was fed up. Enough was enough. He wanted to eat, to pray, to sleep in peace.

During the sirens, they stared together at the TV screen, at a flashing "Danger Ongoing" and then, improbably, at Bugs Bunny screeching, "Of course you realize, dis means war!" They heard CNN announce: "Decapitation Strike." They heard: "Shock and Awe." They heard: "Lit Oil Wells in the South" and "A Circle of Fire."

Amerika spent most of those first few days of the war in her bedroom, stretched out as wide and open as possible on her bed, listening to the sirens sounding endlessly, majestically, one after the other, then the all clear. Time felt suspended, attenuated, an inchworm and a cougar. She kept her box and album beside her, not wanting to forget, not wanting to allow the wailing to blot out everything else. She thought of Acapulco gold and being lit up like a Christmas tree. She wanted to remember laughing her head off and the world as her oyster.

On the ninth night of the war, Amerika decides to go for a walk. There is an imposed curfew, she knows there is. She waits until each member of her family falls asleep one by one (like candles blown out after the kind of party her parents had never hosted, would never host, but that she dreams of hosting one day, welcoming her guests in a silver dress), then goes out anyway. She walks into the night where everything, in its velvetiness, seems possible still. The roads are automatic walkways, the empty country, never before so empty, an airport, a promise of something else, outside the Axis, outside war and vitriol and falling down, down, down with melted, exhausted wings. She walks out in a blue pleated skirt and gray V-neck sweater, her box in her outstretched arms. The album stays behind, the scraps of idioms breadcrumbs home. The country is still, fossilized in the amber light of street-lamps. It is cold, the end of March, desert temperature extremes. She wanders down the lonely walkways, pulled by a magnet. She heads toward the edge of the city, toward the devil and the deep blue sea. Police cars float by and, once, a chemical weapons detector truck with equipment on the flat-bed – jerky rotations, colored lights beeping – tasting the air.

Nobody sees Amerika. Nobody is looking for a girl in the dark with a box and a red scarf around her neck. She pushes on, not really thinking but moving, feeling her body ebbing seaward. She stops at a slice of beach, rocks piled up, a concrete pier. She arrives at a sliver of what it used to be before McDonald's rose upon the broken coast. She dances along the shore, tries to imagine it long once again. She pictures Icarus, Alexander's island, whole, afloat on phosphorescent blue, haloed with snow white waves, a place before sons fell.

Amerika pulls her box to her chest and dances harder, the wind knitting lace with her hair. She twirls and dips and kicks up her heels, always the letter *k* at heart. Out of breath, she stops. She rests on the shore, feeling the sand, shattered crystal, embossing the backs of her thighs. The icy waves approach her toes but never dare to touch. Her right hand on the box at her side, she takes in as much air as her lungs will hold. She rests her eyes for a minute, it could only have been a minute. She thinks about icicles and trees bursting red in autumn, parades and clambakes. She thinks about Archie and making out on the beach. Then she thinks about falling, pale flesh, misty rose. She thinks about firebrick red, burnt sienna, and then plumes of dim gray.

When she opens her eyes she sees a shooting star zooming toward her. She smiles. *Stars in my eyes*. She blinks. It continues toward her. She blinks again. She thinks, *Out of the blue*. There are no sirens. A floating star heading toward the shore. *In the twinkling of an eye*. CNN will say: "Surface-to-Surface." It will say: "Non-Existent Arc." It will say: "Chinese Seersucker" and "Under the Radar." It is missile number thirteen, the only one that makes contact. She thinks, *Into thin air*. Amerika picks up her box, kisses it, turns away from the moving star, and flings it as far away from herself as she can. She hears it explode on the pavement. She hears herself explode. *Painting the town red*.

When they come, they find the contents of Amerika's box, charred, scattered, inexplicable. They find footprints of ballet flats, an invisible dance along the shoreline. They find the residue of loss, the triumph of fury. They find traces of a square peg in a round hole and the end of the future. Amerika's box, Amerika, Radio City Rockette extraordinaire, never a mouse, never evil, into thin air she flies, like a kite.

X

Think of it as a living, breathing organism. A dome like the
gently curved back of a whale, covering just over 22,000
square feet. Its skin, a flexible white membrane, deflecting
the rays of an endless sun, held bravely against incessant
blasts of sand, hardly nudged by gust after gust of hot
wind. Brought to life by waves of air, its arc suspended by
a miracle of strong, steady pulses, it formed what would
quickly become our familiar cocoon. In the early 1980s,
when it first went up, we had no idea what it could possibly
be. We were told, "A new gymnasium," but we had no
viable sense of what an indoor gymnasium was. We were
used to PE outdoors, young enough to shrug off the kind
of heat that today would buckle our knees. We thought
nothing of flinging our sparrow bodies into puffs of air
nearly congealed with dust and sweat. The idea of an
indoor place to exercise would never have occurred to us.
But one morning, we noticed a rectangular hole that
rapidly transformed into a gleaming, near Olympic-size
pool. Another day, we saw that the ground around the
pool and to the right of the pool, the size of two basketball
courts at least, had been surfaced bull-blood red, with
sharp yellow lines designating something no doubt
crucial. Soon after, revolving doors of glass and steel went
up at the corners – four sentinels on alert – and between
the doors, massive air vents or pumps. None of that,

however, could have prepared us for the thick white hide crumpled across the red rectangle, remnants of a skinned giant or two. Nothing could have prepared us for the inflation of that white skin – up, up it went – into a half-bubble of mammoth proportions. Our new gym.

We were brats at the time, most of us protected by the warm, snug shadow of our living, breathing bubble. It bounced away fear. It suspended guilt. It eliminated necessity. It instilled confidence, a slanting kind of innocence. What mattered most was that it seemed to breed choices – a zillion lives to lead, all at once if we wanted, a feast of simultaneity, a gorging on opportunity. That castle in the sky would last about a decade, and, even then, it seems impossible we didn't know, in pinched little recesses somewhere, that it all had to be a mirage, a marshmallow mist. Our white bubble would pop soon enough, worse than any weasel, slamming us down onto the dun sandlot home always was.

~

The

Hidden

Light of

Objects

What strikes us is how serene our mother looks stepping off the plane, the prime minister of our small country waiting to greet her. Nothing fazes her. Not the prime minister. Not the string of parliamentarians angling for photo-ops. Not the frenzied media's nest. Not even us. Everything seems to bleed together for Zaina.

For us everything feels sharp, outlined in black. We remark on the rarity of the clouds in the steel sky. We read them as a sign. We have spent ten years reading signs. It is no surprise that on the day of her release we lose ourselves in a flurry of them. Sparrows precariously balanced on instruments played by the army band brought in for a special welcome. A sliver of obstinate moon at an hour when it long should have moved into someone else's night. Most striking of all, through the sulphuric fumes anyone living in an oil town like Kuwait is familiar with, whiffs of vanilla.

They do not comment on my short white hair or papery skin. They fail to note my quick intakes of breath as I navigate the steps of the plane. They see a mask of calm, my practiced serenity. They cannot hear my irregular heartbeat or feel my brittle bones. I perceive little through the flash of bulbs, the microphones under my nose, the hands thrust into mine. Carefully, I embrace my daughters, three stunning women, almost strangers to me. And my husband Karim, his eyes, like mine, creased with age. I refuse to release my burlap sack, my sole acquisition in a decade. The smell of white cake surrounds me, and I wonder how they have managed it.

There are other signs on that arrival day, but we decide that clouds, sparrows, the moon, and vanilla are signs to be taken for wonders, a string of impossibles signaling that the impossible could happen, has indeed happened. We discuss those four signs at length soon after we arrive home, while she is in the shower, her first shower in a decade. There she is, in our father's bathroom, their bathroom, washing off ten years of captivity. We can hear her.

I am not sure what we expected. The night before her arrival, we were a mix of euphoria and palpitations. My father and my youngest sister, Yasmine, were rapturous and starving, endless platters of food not enough to fill them. But Ghusoon, my other sister, and I were agitated, unable to keep down water. Privately, the two of us fretted over our mother's damage. Ten years a prisoner of war. Had she been starved? Tortured? Had what normally happens to women's bodies in war happened to hers? Would she be the mother who kissed our Band-Aids? We were all too old for that now. When Zaina was taken, Yasmine, only ten, was young enough to need kissed Band-Aids. While she was gone, it was those kisses we

218

remembered most. What we would have given to feel her lips on our scraped skin, our faces, our hair. It was, for ten years, a desire that carved through our bellies like an ulcer. To feel her kisses. To hear her morning songs. That night before her return, Ghusoon, now twenty-five, and I, already thirty, wondered whether she could still be the mother who sang us awake. And we felt guilty for wondering.

We didn't expect the calm mask of her face. We wanted tears and dimpled smiles. When we take her into our arms, we want more to be taken into hers. We feel ourselves clinging to her. It reminds us of the way she had always hung on to us before our trips away to school, to camp, to visit cousins in far-flung places. She always wanted us to go off into the world, already at twelve, at fifteen, to recognize ourselves as independent and as strong as she always was. But at the airport, at the final goodbye, she would cling to us as if our separation were going to be forever, as if our plane were going to plummet. We would be antsy, cruel in our childish insouciance. A plane ride! A ski trip! Off to college! We couldn't get away fast enough. Our mother's hugs were quickly forgotten, her pooling eyes a source of gentle teasing. Now it is all reversed. We cling to her. We cry. We worry she will melt into air. She kisses us back but she doesn't cry. She doesn't cling and we want her to.

In the brief interludes provided by her showers – she takes four in the first four hours off the plane and then one every few hours during the first week – we huddle together, parsing our observations of her. Does she seem happy to be back with us? Does she seem sad? Afraid? Angry? Nothing seems to fit. No word can be stretched enough to cover what we think we perceive.

We watch her especially when we think she isn't looking. Every flicker of eyelid, every unassuming gesture, every ripple of expression. Hope? Anxiety? Despair? On the third day, Yasmine declares: "Defiance." Yes, that comes closest, we think. Defiant but not bitter, seemingly without regret. Our regret is sufficient. Enough regret to fill the belly of a whale, a hollowed-out planet. All that time gone, everything she hadn't seen, would never feel or hear. But, we decide, the missing bits we want her to know about have everything to do with our lives, our time gone by, not hers. We recognize our selfishness, feel guilty about our long ropes of regret.

That first week, we don't talk about her ordeal and neither does she. We don't want to push it. We have decided to give her space and time to figure things out. There is no one around to advise us and I'm not sure we would listen anyway. We want to build a wall around her. No therapists, no counselors, no experts. The politicians are there, of course, for the pictures, the papers, the votes, hoping their florid displays of sincerity will cover up the unresolved POW fiasco. Then there are the inevitable family members and friends, thunderously forthcoming with their congratulations. We can feel her wince and it makes us want to slap them all and send them as far away from her as possible. Well-meaning brothers and solicitous sisters. She embraces them though they were never close. They stay for a while that first day, come back the next, but by the third they are more or less gone, promising to visit again soon, to call. We haven't seen them in ten years. They wouldn't call, we thought, and that was fine with us. But nobody, not the politicians, not the family, not the friends, has any advice for us on how to deal with her return, on how to treat her.

That first week, we try to talk about ourselves. Ghusoon goes first, unwrapping her life layer by layer. Married. Working. As happy as our mother would want her to be. A good man. A good job. No baby yet, but soon, in a year, maybe two. Me, Jinan, next. My slow writing life. Yasmine, still in school, almost done. Zaina's three daughters unfolding their lives for her to see, fresh, clean, upbeat, leaving out the grime. But our father, a broken man, unable to voice his layers of sorrow. She listens and watches, her mask of serenity intact. She listens in absolute silence and we chitter like birds to fill the stillness where her voice should be. We are used to doing that. We have learned to speak to ourselves in her voice. We wonder if she still speaks that way, if she still sees the good in everything. "Luck will find you," she always said. We wonder if ten years could come down to what we are sharing with her. Marriages. Jobs. Degrees. How can we demonstrate what it has taken to get to here? Every joy scalloped with sadness. How can we convey to her the years of deliberation before accepting any man, any job, before making any decision? Every opinion and thought already filtered through her. We figure, surely she must know.

It is like having our mother back from the dead. When she was first taken, I would wake up every night in a panic, wanting to run through the streets to find her, to get her back, to erase this abomination that had blackened our already heavy lives. My heart pounding, I would probe the events of that day again, point by point, a sort of unholy equation that I couldn't get to add up. She had woken at dawn. She had prayed. She had gone down into the kitchen to make herself coffee. She had taken her coffee into the living room. That's

221

where we had found her still warm cup. Something had made her go to the door. We would have heard the doorbell. We would have heard a knock. Something had made her leave her coffee on the table and go to the door. She wasn't supposed to do that. It was too soon to feel safe enough, the streets a mess of retreating soldiers and loamy young heroes looking for glory with guns. It had only been a week since the liberation of Kuwait from Iraq, and it was a novelty to be able to open the front door. I figured my mother, restless after almost seven months stuck indoors, had wanted to exercise her newly regained right to step outside, to leave curtains undrawn, to fling open a window even. It had only been a week, but we had quickly recovered old habits. Curious how bodies slink back into their comforts, their ordinary pleasures. So my mother with her coffee and recovered freedom must have heard something, must have forgotten or pretended to forget the procedures that had kept us safe for seven months: doors bolted, curtains drawn, lights out, down into the basement shelter. Her blue and white robe was missing. Her leather sandals. Early March in her flimsy robe and sandals. This image seared me for a decade. She got those sandals in Greece. There is a black and white photograph, taken unawares, of her and my father stepping off a ferry on one of the islands. They paid for the photo when it was offered to them later because she looked gorgeous, her long brown hair, her white cotton shirt.

When she was abducted my father put out photos of her in every corner of our house. Photos of her when they were first married, of her pregnant, of her at parties, at conference dinners with him. Photos of my mother feeding her beloved birds in the garden. The photos gave my father some solace, but they tortured me. It wasn't that I wanted to forget her. I thought about her every day for ten years, not a day without thoughts of her. But I couldn't, even after a decade, look at pictures of her without slipping into the abyss of guilt and regret. I tried to avoid looking at my father's gallery, not needing pictures of her to remember every little thing. Her freesia smell, her butter skin, the small whisper of lines around her light brown eyes, and, as I got older, an insistent memory of her anxieties, the stresses of her own life she had always tried to keep from us. That first week of her return, as we sit huddled together in the living room, it is the island photo behind her back my eyes keep falling upon. It is easier to focus on that than on my mother in the flesh. A vision in a white shirt on an island in Greece, sandals that would disappear for ten years.

During her second week back, my mother sleeps the sleep of the dead. We can't wake her, hard as we try. She eats only once a day, when she gets up to use the bathroom. She doesn't shower. She doesn't speak a word. She is groggy, drugged by a boundless exhaustion, her head flopping around as she swallows cold broth, tea with as much sugar as we can spoon in. We are scared, unsure what to do, no one to ask for help. Where are the experts? We whisper to each other in her room, never leaving her alone for a second. Is it a slow suicide? Will she ever wake up? Will she ever want to speak again? Ghusoon mentions trauma and elective mutism. We can not picture our mother silent forever.

I have only the faintest recollection of the first weeks back. I remember cradling my burlap sack between my feet. I remember refusing to allow Ghusoon to wash my blue and white robe, needing to maintain the smell of my captivity, at least for a while. I remember drowning in sleep and, when coming up for air, I remember thinking only of the nine others.

Before she was taken our mother was loud, the center of every conversation. She would argue with strangers if she felt she had to, never shirking confrontation, but she would also talk intimately to women at the neighborhood fruit and vegetable stall, joke with people in supermarket checkout lines. Shopkeepers adored her, as did the local ice cream vendors on bicycles, for whom she had bought umbrellas and folding chairs, a small reprieve from the crushing heat. In our insular little country with its ten-foot-high concrete walls fortressing private homes, she was an open, generous oddity. People loved her for it, her wide laugh, her sparkling teeth. They felt privileged to be scolded by her, even more to be included in her easy charm. She elevated their lives for a second and they never forgot it. Anywhere else, she would have been a movie star. Even in Kuwait, in the late 1960s, she had been a glamorous host of some television show. We hadn't heard about this till after she was taken, casually mentioned in one of the many newspaper articles about her abduction, the talk of the town for a while. We asked our father about it, and he confirmed the story. Our young mother, a television queen in her green Alfa Romeo Spider, her endless legs in a mini dress, her brown hair twirling in the wind. It was this Sophia Loren image of her that had compelled our father Karim, a fresh graduate from the University of Vienna medical school, to seek her out, to, as he put it, "Forge my destiny." He knew the kind of life he wanted, and, with the confident certainty of someone who had learned German and Latin in a year, he went after it. So many things about Zaina we didn't know, secrets hidden in other people's pockets, in the objects that belonged to her.

With the exception of her clothes, we didn't have it in us to go through her belongings for the first five years or so. Our father asked us to move her clothes out of their room about six months after she disappeared because he couldn't stop himself from slumping down in her closet, inhaling what was left of her smell. We all did that whenever we thought no one else was around. If for me pictures of her were the hardest residue to bear, for Yasmine it was our mother's smell. For a year or so after our mother disappeared, the unmistakable smell of her clothes, of the inside of her purses, even of her shoes would make my baby sister weep. We would find her asleep on the floors of various closets, hidden under layers of our mother's shawls and dresses, on a bed of her high heels. It was difficult to comfort her, to take her into our arms. She was inconsolable. Maybe she felt our touch as a kind of betrayal. She would allow only our father to carry her back to her small bed, her skinny arms dangling over his shoulders as he whispered things Ghusoon and I couldn't hear.

We worry that our mother feels left out, a foreigner in her own home. *Unheimlich*, our father says to us and to her, a familiarity made uncanny, a home no longer homey. We tried to keep the house exactly as it had been before she was lost to us. Not a thing out of place apart from her clothes, which we put back meticulously when we were informed she was going to be released. We had memorized the placement of every object in our parents' room, in her drawers, closets, cupboards,

225

in the dining room, living room, her kitchen. Her *Betty Crocker Cookbook*. A string of old Kuwaiti pearls given to her by her mother. Her Clinique Nude lipstick. Monogrammed handkerchiefs. Hand-painted champagne flutes. Flower vases from Prague. Her father's books that smelled of India. Her straw hat. Matches collected from restaurants. Her fine Kashmiri shawl, pulled through her wedding ring with a flourish. Boxes of Christmas ornaments on which she had written *Packed by Mom with love*; we could never bring ourselves to open those boxes. Wave-worn stones from Capri. Silver bangles that sounded like wind chimes around her wrists. We went through some of these things over the years, always looking for answers that weren't there. We tried not to allow ourselves to think too hard about the specifics of her absence. We focused on her being alive, not on the conditions of her life away from us. We wrapped ourselves in the familiarity of her things. But now that she is back, we fear that her objects, her rooms, the life she was forced to leave behind are no longer her home. To her, they must be both familiar and unfamiliar. Maybe their familiarity makes her afraid, makes her recognize what she, like us, has taught herself not to see over those ten years. To survive.

Unheimlich. *Karim is right to use that word.* Unheimlich, *precisely. Every one of us had something in that windowless space, gray with unswept dust, that stood for home. For me it was counting objects. Not quite counting them. Naming them, sorting them into categories, telling their histories, and trying to remember where they would be in my house. I would explain it to myself as though I were attempting to give one of my daughters or Karim instructions over the phone to find the thing I needed. "My gray Kashmiri shawl. You know, the one we bought together on our honeymoon from the blind man who said he had spun the yarn for it with his own knotted hands. Remember how he held them out for us to look at? Remember how young we were, believing him to be over a hundred? He was probably forty-five. It's in the chest of drawers on the left-hand side of the bedroom. It's in the last one, under my leather gloves." Or, I imagined myself saying to Jinan, "Habibti, if you go to the closet in the hallway, down in the storage area under the last shelf, you'll find an inlaid wooden box. The key for that box is in a small porcelain bowl in the drawer of my bedside table. Unlock the box and inside it you'll find the tiny emerald ring my father-in-law gave to me when your father and I got engaged. It was the only possession of value his mother brought with her to Basra from Circassia, pressed into her young hands by her father before he sold her off to an Arab merchant who, in turn, sold her to your great grandfather. Struck by her mythical beauty, he quickly married her."*

A litany of objects. My home for a decade.

Before she was taken, my mother was a quietly religious woman, her prayers like goldfish in a Japanese garden pond under a bridge. She prayed five times a day, but she never discussed her faith with her brood of agnostics and atheists. It didn't bother her what we did or did not believe and it didn't bother us that she believed. After she was taken, religion fluttered through the air as an option. We heard from meddling family members that it helped to submit to God's will, to trust that He had a plan for our mother, for us. In the first few shell-shocked days of her abduction, we may have given in to some magical thinking. We would have made a pact with the devil let alone a bargain with God to get her back. It didn't take long to realize that neither would return Zaina to us. Believing in the randomness of events gave us more comfort than any god or devil could. If we had any faith, we put it in the luck of the draw. We wondered whether her beliefs were providing her with sanctuary wherever she was. We wondered whether the things that were happening to her had caused her to lose faith.

Religion was Selma's anchor. The loss of privacy – ten of us packed into a cell too small for five – made it difficult for me to pray. Selma had no such qualms. While I worried my phantom objects like beads on a misbah, *Selma quietly recited her Qur'an. For Khadija it was singing, her husky voice as unexpected in that cell as a hot shower. She was the youngest among us, only twenty, and when she opened her mouth to sing, danger would pour out. Noor had her numbers, strings of equations dancing through her head. Hanan came up with as many palindromes as she could. Altaf used recipes, reciting intricate formulas for the preparation of meals we all longed to eat. Dalal drew portraits of people she knew in the dust on the floors and walls of our cell. Aisha collected insects and trapped them in plastic bottles she managed to secure from the guards. She helped reduce the population of roaches, beetles, and crickets coating our premises. Dana, a poet, puzzled through words, some she shared with us, others she kept to herself. When she felt like it, she would recite Mahmoud Darwish, Abu Nuwas, Adonis, her memory for language*

unfailing. For Hala it was tracing cracks in the walls. Hours
spent following serpentine paths of hairline fissures or major
valleys splitting some of the bricks clean in two. At first she
was looking for points out to freedom. But after a year or so,
she, and we, recognized that there were no gaps in the thick
walls. Still, she didn't stop, her graceful fingers gliding up and
down, her lithe body moving to Khadija's songs.

In these unlikely ways, and together, we survived.

After the week of sleep, my mother speaks. "What you may
think happened, did not." We immediately know what she is
talking about. That ugly violation of the body, that laying
claim over it. She stops there. No further assurances. She is
still on the bed, still under her quilt covers, but no longer
always asleep. She seems suddenly less fragile, less dazed.
Yasmine is right. Our mother seems defiant. Is it directed
against her captors still? We, in our perpetual self-involve-
ment, worry it might be against us. We aren't sure. We want
to believe her. We want her intact, like she was before she was
taken. Unraped. We can't tolerate the desecration of her body.
We can't bring ourselves to think about the forms it could
take, always takes, in war. Could she be the exception after
ten years? Could she have come through unscathed? We want
to believe her, but we think she is lying. We want to tell her
that we will help her through anything, will give her back her
body, will take away the damage. We are, all of us, unprep-
ared, ineffectual. We are, mostly, silent.

The morning I was abducted, what I heard, what drew me to
the front door away from my coffee, was the strangled sound

229

of a woman struggling for air. My instinct was not to warn my family, not to dive down into the basement. It should have been – I have my own tangled ropes of regret. My instinct was to go see. What I saw when I threw open the door was a young woman on her knees with a thick clear plastic bag over her head. Her stricken eyes, jerking desperately in my direction, appeared strangely magnified. Two heavyset men stood over her, pulling the rope around her neck in opposite directions. I heard the snap. They removed the bag. I couldn't take my eyes off her face. I didn't recognize her, but she was somebody's daughter. Before I could react or make a sound, the men swooped down on me, put the same plastic bag over my head – I could smell her saliva, her fear – and stuffed the dead girl and me into the trunk of what I am certain was a stolen Mercedes. I was grateful for the roomy trunk.

They hadn't bothered to tie up my hands or feet, so it was easy enough to pull the bag off my head and push the poor girl into the deepest part of the trunk. I kicked out one of the tail lights with my foot. In that first week after liberation, however, there wasn't anyone around to notice. There were people on the streets all right, but they were too busy doing wrong – looting, exacting revenge on innocents – to pay any attention to me. The car flew through the desert. I don't know how the men managed to bypass undetected all those American troops, but they did, all the way to Baghdad. In the few seconds from when the car stopped to when they opened the trunk, I thought only of my three girls. I expected an immediate pistol to the head and I was trying to blot out fear with images of my babies. They dragged me out of the trunk. My legs would not hold, so they propped me against a wall.

They blindfolded me and tied my hands behind my back. I could hear them yelling to someone named Mohammed to come out for a pickup. They didn't say a word to me and I kept as silent as cotton. I could hear them struggling to remove the girl's rigid body from the car. I anticipated a similar end for myself. Instead, I heard the car doors slam shut and the engine revving up. A squeal of tires and they were gone.

I expected Mohammed to bear down on me at any moment. He didn't. I could feel the warmth of the sun on my forehead, could almost see its orange glow through my closed and covered eyelids. My limbs ached. I tried as hard as I could to escape the binding, unsuccessfully. Hours must have passed. I could feel it getting darker, the cold seeping into my bones. No sign of Mohammed. I fell into an irregular sleep, waking up confused, fingers reaching for Karim's hand the way they often did. After five hours, maybe ten, someone pulled me up by the hair. Mohammed. He pushed me from behind, leading me somewhere. He must have spoken, but I remember nothing of what he said. He removed my blindfold and shoved me into a pitch black hovel, nothing more than a hole in the ground with wood over the top, two small cracks for air. I must have fainted almost instantly because, again, I have no memory of that first time in the hole. All of us spent our first day in the hole, a kind of breaking in, but after that it was rare. When a guard was in a sadistic frenzy, he would shove one of us down in, but, thankfully, that didn't happen often. The hole smelled of river mud, and we had taught ourselves to close our eyes and imagine floating on a raft in blue waters, an endless course of aquamarine. It took discipline, but over time it worked, and the hole, like our cell, couldn't touch us.

There weren't many guarding us, only four or five, and as far as we could tell, we were the only prisoners in the building. It wasn't a conventional prison, we knew that all along, and when we were released, we weren't surprised to find that it was the basement of a quite ordinary villa in a suburb of Baghdad. The guards were all men. This caused exactly the kind of trouble you would expect, especially during the first few years and especially for the lovely Khadija, who has two children to show for it. My daughters suspect I lied when I said nothing happened. It isn't shame that stops me from telling them. We aren't that kind of family, and I was not – am not – that kind of woman. What stops me from telling them right away is something more complicated than shame or guilt or even regret.

There is no going back. I should have realized this after the occupation, the so-called liberation. Nothing, not a thing, went back to the way it had been. New people in the country, new food, new habits, new language. Suddenly, women swathed in ominous black hoods. One year can blot out the past, everything that we were before – twinkling water, pure desert – and life is channeled into a bucket of mud. No going back. The filth and dirt everywhere, the corruption, the sooted skies and murky seas. Nobody seemed to care, everyone swallowing fistfuls of dollars as fast as they could. We were suspended, watching it all through sandblasted glass, thinking everything was different because she had been taken from us, making it personal. But it wasn't just her absence, this new and sadly rotting Kuwait. She would have known how to deal with it, we told ourselves, how to make life work despite the doomed tangle. We were, for ten years, in a situation that was *unheimlich*. We no longer belonged. All we could do was look back and pine for what could never again exist.

Our lives before were padded by her presence. There are people who know how to make life safe despite the deepest sorrows. With a matchbox and Kleenex my mother would fashion baby ghost dolls in a tiny bed for us to play with. And when she and my father had some money, working like demons in their twenties, the early successes of our precious little boomtown, she spent it on travel, on buying beautiful things, on her garden, her house, because she knew it could all disappear, that now was the time to enjoy it. "The thing is to be light as air," she would say. Our lives before were as light as air. We were lucky. Luck of the draw. The lucky are hated the world over, detested, and rightly so. The lucky make it worse for everyone else. But we have paid our dues. So has she and she didn't deserve it.

In the trunk of that still Mercedes, when I believed I would be dead in seconds, thoughts of my girls filled me. It felt like being lit from the inside and the fear of death, though undeniably there, diminished. They go on, I go on. Once it became clear none of us was going to be killed – the small number of Kuwaiti POWs kept alive were, apparently, valuable bargaining chips in the endless negotiation for reduced sanctions or increased loans – I knew something had to change. I could not keep filling myself with their light, my children's or even my husband's, because it made me want to go home, heimlich, *and, as we came to realize after that first year in captivity, there was no chance we were going home any time soon. It*

233

wasn't that I stopped thinking about them completely; that would have been impossible. But what allowed me to create a new kind of home for myself out of the infuriating suspension we now inhabited, a limbo punctuated by the violence and disregard of men whose poverty and desperation could be seen in their bloodshot eyes and crusty yellow nails, was shifting focus from the life I knew to the objects I had once owned. Between my body and me, between the ones I loved and me, a cavalcade of possessions. I can't expect them to understand any of that yet. How the things that belonged to me – fine lace pieces from Burano, clumps of silver jewelry from Peshawar, my youngest daughter's old blanket, red clay pots from Lebanon, my father's dusty books from India, a little packet of playing cards wrapped in the brightest fuchsia tissue paper (which I could never bring myself to unwrap), my mother's string of delicate pearls floating in gold, her gift to me before she died – each in their way embalmed the kernels of my life.

It has been a month now since her release. She walks through the house in a kind of bubble, touching her objects. She wanders from room to room, opens every cabinet, every drawer, touches the lace covering her mahogany tables, the transparent porcelain teacups, the carved wooden duck. She opens her old copy of *One Hundred Years of Solitude*, the one she bought the year I was born, the one in which I had found a black and white photograph of her and my father kissing. Not a kiss others would have been allowed to witness, not the kind of kiss we had always seen them share. This was a private, phantom kiss taken by I don't know who, maybe just my father's camera on a tripod. I see her find that lost

234

photograph one morning, watch her breathe out sharply as it falls from the yellowed pages. She is, I think, trying to account for something. I'm not sure what. We've all lost our bearings now that she is back. The guilt I feel for putting that into words. Sometimes language should fail. We've become ghosts again, like we were the first few years she was gone. In the years since, we built small lives, with guilt, with regret. Does she see it? Now we are suspended again, unable to work, to speak, to think. My father stumbling, trying to make sense of himself with his wife back. She can't help him yet. He can't help her either. She stepped off the plane with a burlap sack. Inside her sack: blue and white robe, Greek island sandals. To see her walking through the rooms in her blue and white robe – the same robe, the same sandals – shocks. We can't make it add up.

I am not defiant. I might wear my intransigence on my sleeve more than before. "The thing is to be as light as air," I used to say. It's what I wanted my girls to learn. To enter the interstices of life like air, like a shawl through a rose gold ring. To be present and, at the same time, to wander through the alleys of the past, plucking memories and possibilities like grapes off vines. A scarf, a ring, a string of pearls. An alternative to the inexplicable anxiety that would sometimes grip me in the best of times, would have me shaking for hours in the bathroom where Karim would find me, coax me through. Burlap sack, leather sandals, blue and white robe. Not to ground me or to weigh me down, but the opposite. To set me free, to give me the strength to remember that, in the end, we all die. I will die. My husband will die. My beautiful girls, one by one, will die.

The thing is to be as light as air in the meantime. I see the three of them now, gazelles with wide fearful eyes. I sense, too, the steel rod running through them. My indelible mark.

The objects. To find them – in their drawers, cabinets, clos-ets, on tabletops, under beds – is an uncanny delight and a heartbreak. They are more familiar to me than my own body. Seeing them again after a decade means more to me than seeing my family. Sometimes language should fail. I wander through this space that cannot yet feel like home, touching the random oddments that kept me alive. Everything is exactly in its place, like I never left. Who was the dogged monitor of this decade-long precision? Jinan? Ghusoon? Surely not Karim, his legendary absentmindedness an impediment, to say the least. Little Yasmine? All of them, in their way, involved in curating this museum of my belongings. As if they knew all along; as if from afar they were trying, so heroically, to save me. Their lives, like mine, suspended, in spite of marriages and schooling and jobs that pay well. Their broken, damaged lives held together by the painstaking placement of objects that belonged to their lost mother. It takes every speck of self-discipline left not to fall to my knees and wail. The bitterest guilt, a paralyzing regret. To pick up an old book with its dry, saffron pages, to see my name and a date inscribed inside the front cover, from so many, many years ago, is to know with the certainty of a sharp slap that time has betrayed us. My conjured objects, frozen under a forgiving layer of ice, were safe, forever preserved. But in the heat of life, books and lace yellow, vases and porcelain chip, and shawls, even magical ones from Kashmir, are easily perforated by moths. No going back.

From the pages of One Hundred Years, *a phantom kiss. Karim and I on our honeymoon on a houseboat in Kashmir. Beneath our feet, water as blue as the blind eyes of the man who sold us the shawl. It strikes me as tragic that he will never see the tremendous, heart-stopping beauty of his homeland. He laughs as he hands me the shawl, as though mocking my unvoiced pity. Our hunger to see everything in the universe is voracious, and we thank the glittering stars above – so impossibly close, we notice, almost near enough to grab – for our eyes, our ears, our noses, our mouths. On a rock as round and smooth as an egg, Karim and I kiss each other hard, like the world itself depends on it. With our eyes closed and our mouths open, we feel what it means to be young, to believe everything is utterly possible. I hadn't noticed Karim's tripod at the time and forgot about that kiss until he showed me the photograph of it months, maybe years, later. I placed it carefully in the pages of my favorite book, never wanting to forget again – in the whirlwind of children and work and habit – the promise of that kiss.*

Ten years interned, a litany of objects, but not this photograph. It falls out now, a lifetime later, forgotten thing. In the smoothness of our skin and the white rock under us, I see the old man, his ancient glacier eyes. A promise to love despite war and unrecoverable time. A way home.

Acknowledgements

Thanks, first, to Andy Smart, without whom, no book.

At Bloomsbury, thanks to Kathy Rooney, for her unstinting support; to Sophia Blackwell, whose generosity extended way beyond her role as publicist; and to Erica Jarnes, for her meticulous attentiveness throughout the process. Thanks to Michelle Wallin, editor extraordinaire, ideal reader.

Thanks to Frances and Andy Lench, for throwing open the doors of Chateau Carignan to members of the Bordeaux Writers Workshop every summer since 2008. Thanks to the brilliant women of the Bordeaux Writers Workshop: A. Manette Ansay, Jean Grant, Frances Lench, Martha Payne, Natalia Sarkissian, Laura Schalk, and Lisa Von Trapp. Many of these stories are better for their discernment and care. Special thanks to Manette, for reading and rereading over the years, for her eyes, both sharp and wise, for her encouragement.

Thanks to the island of Sifnos, for keeping alive what in most other places has disappeared forever, and for taking us in. Many of these pages were written there.

To my sisters, Wijdan, Rania (my first reader), and Farah, thank you for reeling in the crazy and for keeping me fundamentally, despite everything, happy.

Thanks to my parents, for their improbable union, their ease in the world, their unwavering love, and for letting us go. This book is dedicated to them.

Finally, thanks to Adeeb, without whom, nothing.

A NOTE ON THE TYPES

The text of this book is set in Linotype Sabon, named after the type founder, Jacques Sabon. It was designed by Jan Tschichold and jointly developed by Linotype, Monotype and Stempel, in response to a need for a typeface to be available in identical form for mechanical hot metal composition and hand composition using foundry type.

Tschichold based his design for Sabon roman on a font engraved by Garamond, and Sabon italic on a font by Granjon. It was first used in 1966 and has proved an enduring modern classic.